# THE FUGITIVE PAIR

## Matt & Michelle Book 2

## HENRY VOGEL

Published in the United States of America by Rampant Loon Press, an imprint of Rampant Loon Media LLC, P.O. Box 111, Lake Elmo, Minnesota 55042. "Rampant Loon Press" and the Rampant Loon colophon are trademarks of Rampant Loon Media LLC.

www.rampantloonmedia.com

Cover design by goonwrite.com

ISBN: 978-1-938834-83-7 (ebook)

ISBN: 978-1-938834-84-4 (print)

First publication: August 2016

# FUGITIVES ONCE MORE

I kept every sense on high alert as I walked down the path. My eyes scanned everything before me. My ears strained to hear everything behind me. My nose sought for strange and out-of-place odors wafting through the trees. All of my senses concentrated on the task at hand—yet I fought to keep my empathic ability focused on rooting out malicious intent. And it was a major struggle.

My mental filters slipped and slid around in my head, knocked askew by random sights, sounds, and smells. Once the filters were even slightly out of place, unwanted emotions crashed in from all around me, intruding on my thoughts. The simple joy of a gentle breeze on a face. The first gnawing of late afternoon hunger pangs. Casual lust at the sight of a pretty girl.

Wait! I didn't have any pretty girls in my field of vision. I brought my filters back under control and zeroed in on the lusty thoughts. I spotted the guy sitting on a bench about ten meters ahead of me. His gaze wandered a bit but always swung back to look behind me. Concentrating hard, I slammed all of my filters back in place then quickly pulled out the filter for menace.

And that's when I picked her up, sashaying up the path as pretty as you please and looking like nothing more than a girl

1

enjoying being out and about on such a lovely day. But I knew she was on the prowl, with me playing the part of the prey. I couldn't begin to guess *what* she planned to do to me—empaths only pick up emotions, not detailed thoughts—but knowing *who* was targeting me gave me the advantage.

I slowed down and turned my gaze up into a tree but kept my psychic attention trained on the girl. Judging distance based on emotional feedback isn't easy, but I've been practicing. I waited for the slight uptick in the intensity of the girl's emotions heralding the change from intent to action.

I never caught the change. Something hit me in the chest with a quiet pop. Looking down, I found red paint splattered right over my heart. Looking up, I saw Jonas, head of my security detail and my father-in-law, watching me over the barrel of a paint gun from thirty meters away.

"You're dead, Matt," Jonas called, walking toward me.

"Do I at least get partial credit for picking up Michelle coming up behind me?"

My wife's arms snaked around me and hugged me from behind. She rose up on her toes and breathed into my ear, "I'll give you some credit tonight—but I don't think Daddy will cut you the same slack."

Michelle was mostly right.

"You can't be partially dead so you don't get partial credit." Then Jonas relented and gave a nod. "Still, you're getting better. I was surprised when I realized you had managed to pick up Michelle coming up behind you. It looks like you're getting better at holding your filters in place."

I wanted to accept that little bit of praise, but we were working on potentially life-and-death skills. I shook my head. "Not really, Jonas. My filters slipped and I picked up a few random emotions," I pointed at the man sitting on the bench, "including Tendack's as he ogled a pretty girl."

Michelle crossed her arms and turned a glare on Tendack. "Fantasizing about the boss's wife, Tendack?"

2

The man on the bench reddened slightly but grinned into Michelle's glare. "No, ma'am. I was just sitting here in the park watching for pretty girls. Imagine my surprise when the first one to walk by turned out to be you."

"We're still on the estate grounds, Tendack," Michelle growled, but her smile took all the menace out of it.

"Anyway," I continued, "since I couldn't see any pretty girls, I knew Michelle had to be sneaking up behind me."

"Sneaking?" Michelle protested. "I was just watching your cute ass."

"So I concentrated my ability behind me and picked up my beautiful-but-deadly wife." I met Jonas's eyes and shrugged. "So I didn't exactly pick Michelle out of the crowd on my own."

Jonas surprised me by bestowing a smile on me. "You're downplaying some good work on your part, Matt. You used the information around you and read the situation fairly accurately. The problem came when you concentrated entirely on Michelle and missed my approach and my malicious intent."

Jonas turned and waved in the rest of the security team, signaling an end to this training session. "So, not exactly great on your part—you did end up dead, after all—but not bad, either. You've made some real progress over the last eight months."

I shook my head. "It just seems like it's coming so slowly. I mean, I went from holding my ability in check to finding Michelle floating in space in a matter of minutes."

"Life and death motivate us in ways training just cannot simulate." Jonas wrapped an arm around Michelle's shoulders and gave her a quick hug. "Given the choice, I prefer a slow and frustrating approach to training you. After all, someday my daughter's life might depend on your mastery of those psychic abilities."

I slipped an arm around Michelle's waist, trapping her between us. "And I agree with you, Jonas. I just wish I was making better progress."

Jonas released Michelle and studiously looked away from the two of us. "Mentioning progress, have you managed to figure out how you're able to broadcast your emotions to Michelle when...Ah..."

"When we're making love?" Michelle piped up brightly. When Jonas didn't respond, she said, "Okay, not the phrase my father wants to hear from his daughter. Maybe you'll like 'having sex' better?" Jonas's cheeks actually reddened slightly at that and Michelle's grin turned wicked. "Not that, either. Hm, does that mean 'screwing' is out, too?"

I took pity on Jonas and interrupted Michelle. "I'm sorry, Jonas, but learning how I project my emotions to Michelle during our most, um, intimate moments takes concentration—and my concentration is on Michelle and not on what my ability is doing."

"And it had better stay that way, babe," Michelle added.

"I know what I'm asking is difficult, Matt," Jonas replied, the red fading from his cheeks. "God knows I remember when Magda and I were newlyweds. I wanted to please her so much—"

"Whoa, whoa, whoa!" Michelle cried. "Daughter present who doesn't want to hear about her parents' sex life."

Now it was Jonas's turn to grin wickedly. "What? After your list of phrases, I'd have thought—"

"You thought wrong, Daddy dear, and I've grown tired of this topic."

Jonas lifted his hands in mock surrender. "Okay, Michelle, you win. So, I guess I shouldn't suggest Matt try projecting his emotions to you as part of foreplay?"

"*Daddy!*"

"Jonas, dear, are you torturing our daughter?" My mother-in-law, Magda, was dressed to the nines and standing in the doorway to our house. It used to be the guest house, but Mom and Dad gave it to Michelle and me after we rescued them from pirates.

"Are we running late for our dinner date?" Jonas checked the time. "Besides, she started it."

Magda shook her head. "I haven't heard that excuse since the two of you held tickle fights when Michelle was six." She held up her watch and tapped it. "Our reservations are in one hour, all three of you need to shower and change clothes, and this little house only has two showers."

Michelle took my hand and led me off toward our bedroom. "No problem. Matt and I can shower together."

As we disappeared into the bedroom, Magda sighed. "I'll call the restaurant and tell them we're going to be late."

My mother-in-law was right. We were late.

Even after eight months of marriage to his daughter, I still found it odd watching Jonas in a domestic setting. I'd only known him as my chief of security and, on those occasions when I wanted to sneak off on my own, my diabolical arch-nemesis. In my mind, guarding me encompassed his whole life. I had imagined him living in a small efficiency apartment which was short on luxuries because Jonas was all business. Then came that fateful night when my foolishness forced Jonas to call on Michelle—the secret body-guard I never knew I had—to rescue me from hired thugs intent on killing me. In the span of five minutes, Jonas morphed into a family man with a wonderful wife and a daughter who just happened to be the love of my life.

"The repulsers on my car have drifted out of alignment, Jonas," Magda said, taking a delicate bite of her steak.

Jonas, his mind obviously elsewhere, said, "Mm hm."

Magda gave Michelle and me an exasperated look then grinned. "There's just enough wobble that I can't drive naked from the hood of the car anymore."

Chewing mechanically, Jonas answered the same way. "Is that so?"

"Yes, dear, and now I can't teach Michelle how to do it. She's very disappointed."

Michelle snorted, failing to completely smother her laughter, while I marveled at the strange ways new fantasies are born.

"That's a pity, dear."

Michelle's mother caught Jonas's hand and shook it. "Dear heart, could you please join us for dinner or, at the very least, tell us what has you so distracted?"

Jonas's eyes focused on his wife and he gave a tight smile. "I'm sorry, Magda. Work stuff. I'll try to pay better attention."

"We haven't been out to dinner with Michelle and Matt in over a month, Jonas. Considering they *are* your work, perhaps you could pay more attention to them? Unless you'd like to share what's distracting you?"

"I'd prefer not to discuss it in such a public location. You never know who might be eaves—"

"Oh, look! It's Matt and Michelle." The voice came from behind us, so the speaker didn't see the pained look cross Michelle's face and mine when we recognized it. "Why don't we see you at the clubs anymore, Michelle?"

Jayna, the prettiest and least personable girl in our school walked over to the table. Brenda, second only to Jayna in both categories, trailed along. The two girls wore skirts so short I was surprised they weren't mooning half the restaurant and shirts whose necklines plunged to their navels.

Michelle plastered on a smile just as warm and genuine as the ones Jayna and Brenda wore. "I'm married now, Jayna. Maybe you heard about it? Some people say it was part of last summer's biggest news story."

"Just because you're married doesn't mean you have to give up clubbing. Married girls can still go dancing. I suppose you can even bring *him* along." I found myself on the receiving end of a laser-hot stare from Jayna. "He'll cut into your action, but—"

Michelle looped an arm through mine and leaned against me. "I already get all the action I desire."

Brenda snorted. "You must not desire much, Michelle. Jayna was there before you and she told me good old Matt is about as clueless as they come."

I grinned at Brenda. "That's because I never wanted Jayna. I only dated her to make Michelle jealous."

Jayna's eyes bugged out and her mouth opened and closed a few times without anything coming out. I liked the look, but Brenda spoiled the moment by finding her voice.

"Don't be ridiculous, Matt. Jayna is more beautiful than Michelle."

"Yes, Jayna is beautiful—just like a perfectly wrapped empty box." I shook my head in mock pity. "Wrapping paper is all you get. Once you get past it there's nothing left to discover."

"You have got to be joking, Matt." Brenda ran a hand from her neck to her navel. "Unwrapping me is all guys ever care about. Well, unless the guy is an idiot like *you*. I mean seriously, what has Michelle got that Jayna and I don't have?"

"A brain." That earned me a sensuous kiss from Michelle. I didn't even need a psychic ability to figure out the kiss was a promise for more when we got home.

As Michelle and I finished the kiss, my mother-in-law smiled at the two interlopers. "You're obviously Jayna, so you just *have* to be Brenda. Michelle told me all about you two." Magda turned her smile on Michelle. "It appears I owe you an apology, dear."

Jayna and Brenda exchanged puzzled looks. Equally confused, Michelle asked, "What do you mean, Mom?"

"I always assumed you were exaggerating when you talked about these two." Magda shook her head gently. "You're right, Michelle. They really do put the bitch in the phrase rich bitch."

As Jayna and Brenda sputtered, Jonas rose and took each girl by an elbow. "I think you girls have overstayed your welcome. Come along."

Jonas steered the still-sputtering girls to the door. He exchanged a few words with the manager, who escorted the pair the rest of the way out of the restaurant under Jonas's watchful eye.

As Jonas sat, Michelle asked, "What did you say to the manager, Daddy?"

"Hm? Oh, I just told him Mr. and Mrs. Connaught felt those two had overstayed their welcome."

"Surely the manager noticed that my parents aren't even here, Jonas," I said.

Magda patted my hand. "Jonas was referring to you and Michelle."

I blushed. "Oh yeah. I'm still getting used to that mister and missus bit. But that still doesn't explain why the manager threw Jayna and Brenda out."

"You own this restaurant, Matt," Jonas said. "Actually, your family owns the company which owns it, but it amounts to the same thing."

"Oh. I guess I need to spend more time learning all of my family's holdings. But why did you drag Jayna and Brenda to the door? You could have just called for the manager."

Jonas's lips compressed into a frown. "I wanted an excuse to take a look outside."

"Is that why you were so distracted a few minutes ago, dear?" Magda asked.

Jonas nodded. "The security team outside the restaurant reported a suspicious vehicle parked right outside the door. The team is running the plates but I think Matt should check for threats."

Michelle took my hand and turned troubled eyes on her father. "Do you think they're working for Matt's uncle?"

"I dearly wish they were, pumpkin, but I think the car belongs to the Federation government. If they're looking for us, it's almost certainly Psi Corps."

My heart leapt into my mouth. "How——?"

"Before we start worrying needlessly, please find out if they're here for you, Matt." Jonas gave me one of his rare smiles and his voice assumed the more formal tone he used with me before I married his daughter. "I'm not going to let anything happen to you, sir."

Magda patted Michelle's hand. "Perhaps you ought to help Matt open up."

Michelle tore her gaze from me and looked at her mother. "What?"

"Kiss him like you two are back home and tearing each other's clothes off."

"Mom!" Michelle's cheeks reddened slightly, but then she took my head in her hands and did just as her mother suggested.

My mind was whirling and, from the tentative way Michelle kissed me, hers was, too. Gradually, our desire for each other pushed other thoughts of our minds.

"Read the area," Michelle breathed into my ear.

My mind opened up and I read the emotions from those all around us. Our kiss drew the attention of nearby diners, whose reactions ranged from amusement to nostalgia to disdain. Farther away from us, I picked up a wide range of emotions, though nothing unreasonable from patrons at an expensive restaurant. Expanding my read, I picked up the familiar alertness from the security team outside, this time tinged with concern. And then I found the object of the team's concern.

Four people close together and with a strong unity of thought. Alert, calm, and determined, the four people waited for one particular person to emerge from the restaurant—me.

I broke the kiss. "I can't say if they're Psi Corps, Jonas, but they're waiting for me."

"Understood, sir." Jonas stuck to the formal tone, perhaps hoping its familiarity would calm me—which it did. "Michelle, I had one of the men bring your Jusair in case we needed to split up. It's parked in an alley behind the restaurant. While you and Matt leave through the kitchen, your mother and I will go out the front and pretend to wait by our usual car for the two of you to join us. With any luck, that will distract the people looking for Matt and give you two a chance to escape."

Michelle turned all business, matching her father's tone. "Did the security team spot anyone else suspicious in the area?"

"No, but you should assume they have backup within a block of the restaurant. I also recommend you wear your wig and keep Matt out of sight until you're well away from here."

"Will do, Daddy. Where do you want us to go?"

Jonas hesitated for a second. "Take a circuitous route toward the Promenade. I have a decoy set up near there. We also have a spaceship docked near there. It's already fueled and fully provisioned."

Magda paled. "Do you think it's that bad, Jonas?"

"I hope not, but I also want Matt and Michelle prepared if it is."

Without another word, Michelle and I got up and walked to the back of the restaurant. The manager met us there and escorted us through the kitchen. He motioned for us to hang back as he opened the backdoor and checked the alley. Then he gave us a nod and we slipped into the alley.

Michelle's green Jusair was parked right outside the door. Michelle slid into the driver's seat as I ran around the car and hopped into the passenger seat. My wife popped open a compartment on the dashboard and pulled out a long black wig.

As she flipped the wig over her head, Michelle said, "Lay your head in my lap and stay down whatever happens. We're coming out onto the street within thirty meters of the people looking for you."

I did as instructed—usually something I'd find enjoyable—and tried to slow my racing heart as Michelle drove toward the mouth of the alley. She touched the com button on the dashboard. Jonas answered immediately.

"Where are you?"

"Approaching the mouth of the alley. It's time for you and Mom to leave the restaurant."

"We're going through the doors now. All eyes in the government car are looking at us."

Seconds later, Michelle stopped the car and her head swiveled back and forth as she checked traffic before pulling out onto the street. With a sharp intake of breath, she muttered, "Dammit, no. Not now!"

"What is it?" Jonas asked over the com.

In answer, I heard a knock on the car's window followed by Jayna's loud voice. "So you decided to ditch boring old Matt and go clubbing with us? You do know you look ridiculous in the wig, Michelle?"

Over the com, Jonas said, "The government team just spotted you, Michelle. Go. Now!"

Michelle pushed the throttle to the floor and the little Jusair shot out into the street. Horns blared as cars braked to avoid hitting us. Then more horns sounded down the street as the Federation car accelerated after us. I checked the rearview cam. The Federation car drew closer by the second.

"The Feds are catching up fast, Michelle." I gave up on the cam and craned my neck to look out the back window. "I don't think we can outrun them in a little car like this."

A feral grin spread across Michelle's face. "Babe, do you really think Daddy would send his little girl out in anything as lame as a standard Jusair? Especially when I might have to use it to get you to safety?"

"Um, no?"

"I've been waiting *years* for a chance to open this baby up. Make sure your seat belt is buckled tight and hang on honey—things are about to get interesting."

Never let it be said I don't listen to my wife. I checked my belt then grabbed a strap hanging next to my seat. I had just enough time to wonder if the strap was original equipment before Michelle flipped open a compartment on the steering wheel. She pressed the recessed button within.

I sank back into the seat as the car rocketed forward. Our speed doubled within seconds. Rather than fight the acceleration to look out the back window, my eyes returned to the rearview cam. The Fed vehicle shrank on the screen and disappeared as Michelle whipped the Jusair through traffic and other cars blocked the view. We flew past the knot of traffic and into a clear stretch on the road. Seconds later, the Fed car—now running with blinking emergency lights—repulser-hopped over the front row of cars and into the same stretch of clear road.

"Crap, they're keeping up with us," Michelle snarled. "Matt, see if you can get Daddy on the com so we can coordinate with his response teams."

I caught the flash of movement in the corner of my eye. "Look out!"

Two more Federation cars shot out of cross-streets and blocked the street ahead of us. Even before the big cars came to a stop, Michelle thumbed another button on the steering wheel. The whine of the Jusair's repulsers deepened to a rumble and the little car popped ten meters into the air, clearing the roadblock easily. We settled back to the ground and Michelle cut the wheel to the left, taking a side street. The pursuing car sailed over the roadblock, too, staying on our tail as the others scrambled to join the chase.

I managed to drag my attention away from the chase and bring up the car's com. "We're not getting a com signal, Michelle."

"That's bad—the Feds don't shut down com towers for just anyone. They must really want to keep you isolated." Michelle slewed into an intersection, fighting the controls to take a hard left turn. With a jerk, she straightened the car and we zoomed back in the direction of the restaurant, just one street over from it. "Hit the blue button on the com. That'll shift from com to radio."

I did as she instructed and Jonas's voice sprang immediately from the speaker. "—you there? Repeat, Matt or Michelle, are you there?"

"We're here, Jonas," I replied.

"Before you do anything else turn on GenCo encryption. You know the channel."

Jonas assigns a new emergency encryption channel every morning. Michelle says he selects the channel by rolling dice, ensuring something completely random and not generated by anything electronic and, therefore, potentially hackable. I dialed in today's code.

Once we established we were on the same channel, Jonas said, "Report."

"We're heading south on Benton, coming up on Thess now." We flashed through the intersection against the traffic signal. Horns blared in our wake. "Correction, we just passed Thess."

"Why are you coming back this way?" Jonas asked.

"They tried to cut us off with two more cars. I hopped them, but I don't have enough charge to do that many more times. I thought doubling back might buy us a few extra seconds before those two found out which way we went," Michelle answered.

"Okay, there's nothing we can do about that now. I've alerted the decoy team to be ready. They're on the second level of the parking deck next to the Promenade. Can you get there or should I have them move?"

"I can make it." Michelle paused to check the rearview cam for the Fed cars. The first one was no more than a hundred meters behind us. Much farther back, we saw the other two Fed cars make repulser-hops. "Daddy, does all of this mean what I think it means?"

When Jonas replied, his tone was gentle. "I'm afraid so, pumpkin. I've been in communication with the house and the Feds have a team there, too. That's one reason they took down the com towers. I think they're hoping you'll decide this is a simple kidnapping attempt and run for home—and right into the arms of their waiting team. We've got to assume the Feds know about Matt's ability."

Michelle slowed a bit and turned right at the next cross street. The signal was with us this time, so we found another short stretch of clear road ahead of us. Instead of accelerating, Michelle hit the brakes and spun the wheel hard to the right. The Jusair spun around, pointing back the way we came. Michelle downshifted and pushed the throttle to the floor. The car shuddered for a second, and then accelerated back the way we came.

The closest Fed car slid around the corner ahead of us, bouncing off of the line of cars waiting for the signal to change. I watched the other driver fight to regain control as the rear end of the car swung back and forth. Michelle twitched her wheel to the left and zipped past the Fed car with less than a meter to spare. Ahead, the signal changed and a wall of traffic started across the intersection—directly at us.

Michelle swung to the right, nearly sideswiping the same car the Feds hit. I got a glimpse of the driver, his face a mixture of fear and outrage, as we flew past. Without a second thought, Michelle cut back to the left, across lanes filled with approaching traffic. Horns sounded, cars braked, and we heard the grinding sound of metal on metal. Just when a collision looked unavoidable, Michelle thumbed the hopper and the Jusair once again flew up over the oncoming cars, cutting the corner back toward Benton. We cleared the line of southbound cars waiting for the traffic signal and landed in the northbound lane of Benton. My wife straightened the car and sped up the clear stretch of Benton.

Michelle's timing was perfect. We shot past the other two Fed cars in mid-hop and heading in the completely wrong direction.

"We've lost our tails—at least for a few minutes, Daddy," Michelle said. "What do you want us to do when we get to the Promenade parking deck?"

"The decoy car will make an ostentatious exit from the deck which should draw the Feds after it. You should find an out-of-the-way parking spot and ditch the car. There's a pack in the backseat with new clothes and new identities for you. Change clothes and take a leisurely walk on the Promenade."

"You want us to head to that new ship you told us about, Daddy? A spaceship off-planet seems like our best bet right now."

"I agree," Jonas said, "but we've got to get the Feds off your tail before you can go to it."

Michelle spun the wheel right and took the next side street we saw, then turned left at the next intersection, putting us back on the same street where the chase began. "We've got a straight shot to the Promenade. Warn the decoys we'll be there in three minutes."

"Roger that." The channel went silent for a few seconds as Jonas spoke to the decoy team. "Okay, pumpkin, they'll be ready for you."

"So, what do Matt and I do after we take this walk on the Promenade?"

"Take a taxi to the space dock south of the city. Go to docking bay AA23 and use the same key code Matt used to open the pirate bay doors on Pegasus Station. Matt's father bought the ship through half a dozen cutouts, so there's no way to tie it back to GenCo or the two of you."

Half a kilometer behind us, the three Fed cars roared around the corner and back onto our tail. Michelle immediately abandoned the comparatively sedate speed she'd adopted when we returned to this street and was soon weaving around traffic at breakneck speed.

I wanted Michelle concentrating on her driving, so took up the conversation. "Okay, we go to this new spaceship and just take off. Is it safe to assume you've got a flight plan filed?"

"Of course."

"What about alternate signal transponder codes?"

"Really, sir, must you ask?" Jonas actually sounded slightly offended, enough so to stop using my name.

"Yes. You taught me to never assume anything."

Magda's laugh came over the radio. "He's got you there, dear heart."

We were less than a kilometer from the Promenade parking deck and Michelle had more traffic to dodge. The three Fed cars were closing the gap, but the nearest one was still several hundred meters behind us.

"One last question, Jonas," I said. "Where should we go in the spaceship?"

"I...don't know, sir." Jonas sounded unsure of himself. That scared me more than anything else we'd faced so far. "For that matter, I don't *want* to know."

Michelle swung into the approach for the parking deck and, briefly clear of traffic, gunned the engine back to top speed.

"What does that mean, Jonas?"

"It means, sir, you'll be safer if none of us know where you are. Your father has already got company lawyers working on this situation. I'll use one of Michelle's message drops when it's clear for you to come home."

Michelle braked hard as we entered the parking deck. As we disappeared into the gloom of the deck, the three Fed cars turned onto the approach road. Ten seconds later, a Jusair identical to ours sailed into view as it passed over the three Fed cars. I guessed the decoy hopped the railing from the second level. Well, Jonas *did* say it would be ostentatious.

As the three Fed cars spun about and set off in pursuit of the decoy, Michelle parked her car in a dark corner in an underground level of the deck. We changed clothes quickly. Michelle pinned her hair up and pulled a ball cap over her blond hair. I put on a matching cap and we grabbed our new identifications.

"Daddy, Mom, Matt and I are leaving the car."

"I love you, pumpkin," Jonas said. "Matt, take care of my little girl."

"Always, Jonas. And she'll take care of me. Tell my parents I love them."

"They already know that, Matt," Magda said, "but we'll tell them. Go with our love, both of you."

"We love you, too," Michelle said, then flipped off the radio.

My wife and I climbed from the car and headed for the Promenade. Hand-in-hand, we left behind everything we knew and everyone we loved.

The walk through the Promenade was far too long. We walked sedately, arm-in-arm as you'd expect from young lovers. Each time someone came up behind us, I feared the feel of a grasping hand on my shoulder. Each time someone appeared before us, I feared the sight of a drawn weapon. Michelle's usually carefree, swaying body was tense and stiff as a board. I felt certain we stood out from the crowd as surely as if a sign reading 'Fugitives' hovered over our heads.

The walk through the Promenade was all too short. Windborne ocean scents mixed with the familiar smells of the food vendors, combining into a heady aroma which my brain interpreted as home. And for the last eight months, the city truly *was* home. It was a place filled with family and love and joy. It was the one place in the galaxy where I most wished to stay. But now home was the one place in the galaxy where I could not stay. Every step I took was one step less I could take in my home city and on my home world.

Even held under tight rein, my empathic power could always read Michelle. She felt as I did, with the added fear she held for me. I tried to think of something to say to allay her fears, but my mind came up blank. Instead, I simply tried to broadcast my love to her—just as I somehow managed to do during our most intimate moments.

Michelle laid her head against my shoulder briefly. "Same here, babe."

"Why did you say that?"

"Hm? I was..." Michelle bit her lip, a sure sign she was trying to figure something out. "I don't know. It just felt like the right thing to say. Why?"

"I wanted to say something to make you feel better, but words failed me. So I tried broadcasting my love."

Michelle smiled weakly. "We knew you could do it. Daddy would be so proud of you. Just like I am."

"I only wish I could feel better about finally succeeding, but with everything going on..." A truly horrible thought crossed my mind. "What if I can only broadcast when I'm feeling depressed?"

Michelle tightened her arm around me. "Do you get depressed making love to me?"

"You already know the answer to that, Michelle."

"I do. I'm just making sure *you* know the answer, too. Because that's when we discovered you could broadcast." Michelle met my gaze with such intensity that I couldn't have looked away if I'd wanted to. "So you most definitely do *not* have to be depressed to do it. Right?"

"Right. Sorry. I won't forget it again." I stopped walking, leaned over, and kissed Michelle lightly on the lips. "I promise."

As we broke apart, an elderly couple came around each side of us, joining hands as they came back together in front of us.

"Pardon us," I said. "We didn't mean to block the way."

The man turned and smiled. "Don't you worry. It does my heart good to see a young couple in love. When I go walking with a pretty girl, I *always* kiss her."

With that, the man leaned over and kissed the woman walking next to him.

"You old scamp," the old woman said. "What will my husband think?"

He kissed her again. "He approves."

The man gave us a wink and the pair strolled off.

"That'll be us in about a hundred years," Michelle declared.

"Yep."

We both grinned, realizing we each believed we'd be together a century from now. Neither of us knew how we were going to deal with our current problems, but we just assumed we would. Our steps a bit lighter than they'd been mere seconds before, Michelle and I resumed walking. Twelve minutes later we flagged down a taxi. We got out of the cab at the gate for the space dock and walked to docking bay AA23. I coded us into the spaceship and we got our first look at our new home.

From the outside, the ship was nothing more than a Nebula runabout. My first stop inside the ship was the engine room. Even though I was expecting an engine upgrade, I was relieved when I laid eyes on a pair of top-of-the-line starfighter engines. It's illegal to use those in civilian craft but, if the number of smugglers and pirates using military engines is any example, the law is nothing more than a technicality. The weapon systems, barely adequate on a base Nebula, were also replaced with military-grade lasers and a missile launcher. All of the weapons were hidden behind sliding hatches in the ship's hull. Our little ship could run like a rabbit and fight like a fox.

My father and Jonas had stocked the ship well—a wide range of clothing styles for both of us, plenty of food, a full fuel tank, and about a hundred million credits on a range of credit sticks. They thoughtfully included a credit transfer machine so we could move the credits between sticks. Nothing draws attention faster than a couple in their early twenties carrying around credit sticks with seven-figure balances. They'd even filed a standing flight plan, requiring only a simple notification to flight control to activate it.

I settled into the pilot's chair and submitted the notification, requesting the soonest open launch window. Michelle took the navigator's seat just as the flight control computer approved our request. Our designated launch time was in twenty minutes.

"Have you got a destination in mind, Matt?"

"Not really. I was going to discuss it with you during the wormhole jump." I watched Michelle tapping keys on her control board, intently watching the results scroll past. "Have you got a suggestion?"

"Maybe..." She finished tapping keys and smiled at the final results. Leaning back, she pressed a button, sending the results to my screen. "I think we should go to Wolf."

Looking at the chart Michelle sent to me, I said, "Well, it's definitely an out-of-the-way system. I count six jumps and two weeks of travel time following the winding route you chose— which is much better than the direct route through the Piscain Hub. I like your plan of avoiding Federation naval bases. But why Wolf?"

"Three reasons. You've already gotten the first one—it's one of the most remote colonies in Federation space. Beyond Wolf all you have are the fringes, the Federation border, and the unaligned frontier worlds." Michelle held up two fingers. "Second, it's a wormhole crossroads with five different wormholes in the system. The exits for two of those wormholes lie well beyond the Federation border, which could be handy if we have to make another run for it."

Michelle fell silent for a moment, so I prompted, "And the third reason?"

"It's got the most remote Psi Corps office in the Federation."

"Aren't we trying to *avoid* the Psi Corps, babe?"

"Yes, but to what end?" Michelle took my hand and captured my eyes with her own blue ones. "If we don't do something about this situation, we'll never be that old couple walking hand-in-hand on the Promenade."

"I concede the point, but what can we do?"

"In the long run, we spearhead a movement to repeal the psychic impressment laws. In the short run, we've got to figure out a way for you to beat the psychic evaluator."

"That's great in theory," I conceded, "but we can't figure out how to beat the evaluation when we don't know how the evaluator works."

"That's why we need a planet with a Psi Corp office, Matt." Michelle grinned. "We're going to steal an evaluator."

# A WOLF IN SHEEP'S CLOTHING

Sixteen days after slipping away from Draconis, Michelle and I landed on Wolf. While our spaceship had the feel of a refuge from our troubles with Psi Corps and the Federation government, it was far too small to make a comfortable one. Let me tell you, no matter how desperately you love someone, being forced to spend two weeks cooped up with each other—and *only* each other—can really rub your nerves the wrong way at times.

Michelle and I had our first real fight on the fourth day, our second on the seventh day, and two more before reaching Wolf. Don't get me wrong, the make-up sex was fantastic—and that's saying a lot if you know just how amazing empathic sex already is —but even newlyweds like Michelle and me can't spend sixteen days making love.

Our parents did their best to stock the spaceship with entertainment for us. We had favorite vids from our childhood, thousands of books, exercise equipment, and a stasis unit filled with the best food money can buy. I got Michelle as thoroughly hooked on the cheesy *Star Ranger* series as I was, and I found myself hanging on every twist and turn in a ridiculous romance series she loved. But, like the sex, you can only binge on vids for so long.

In other words, we were both thrilled to get off the still-unnamed spaceship, breathe fresh air, and enjoy the wide-open spaces you can only find on a planet. And boy did Wolf have a lot of open space. The spaceport was on a plateau just outside of the planet's capital city, Pacrun. We had a great view of it as I drove our rented ground car—one with wheels, no less—down to the city.

"Wolf's been settled for over a hundred years and *that* is the largest city on the planet?" Michelle asked. "It's teeny tiny. It can't have more than forty or fifty thousand people living there."

"Draconis's capital was half that size a century after Draconis was settled," I said. "We covered all of that in the Draconis history class in school. Don't you remember?"

"I'm sure a smart guy like you can figure out the answer to your own question, Matt," Michelle responded. She made a show of pulling her chrono out and watching it. "In. Ee. Time. Now."

"I don't know what I'm supposed to figure out, babe. Every school kid on Draconis takes planetary history in the fifth—." That's when the realization hit me. "You didn't join our class until the sixth grade."

"Very good, Matthew. And I didn't take Draconis history because...?"

"You lived on Earth until your father came to work for my father."

"There, I knew you could figure it out, Matt."

"Patronizing snarkiness is not your best tone of voice, dear," I said.

"You know, it took me years to forgive my father for taking me away from all my friends on Earth and dragging me to Draconis. As if that wasn't bad enough, he stuck me in the same school with Jayna and Brenda and all those other rich kids." Michelle shook her head as if she still regretted the move.

"Hey, *I* was one of those rich kids."

"And you're the reason why I finally forgave Daddy for taking the job protecting you." Michelle leaned over and snuggled. "So it all turned out for the best—even if I did miss Draconis history in the fifth grade."

We picked a mid-range hotel and checked in, getting a minor surprise in the process.

"Mr. and Mrs. Scott Chambers?" the middle-aged clerk asked. He used a rather archaic form of address since I'd signed us in as Scott and Nicole Chambers. You sometimes run across that kind of thing out on the edge of the Federation, so I just went with it.

"That's us," I said.

"I'll need to see proof of your marriage, otherwise I can't allow the two of you to stay in the same room," the clerk said. His tone was brisk yet challenging as if he expected an argument.

"Is that some kind of local law?" Michelle asked as we pulled out our ID cards and presented them to the clerk.

"It's part of the colonial charter," the clerk responded, his tone simply brisk now that he realized we weren't going to argue with him. "A colony world can't afford the kind of support services you've got on..." He checked our IDs. "A world like Draconis. The colony set out some pretty strict policies about marriage, so children always had two parents taking care of them."

Handing the IDs back to us, the clerk added, "A young couple like you can't have been married very long. Is this your honeymoon?"

"We've been married for about eight months, so this isn't really a honeymoon," I said.

"Even though it *is* the first time we've gotten away from both sets of parents since the wedding," Michelle added.

The clerk gave a knowing nod. "Both of your parents sound a lot like my wife's parents. We had to move to the city to get free of their influence." He checked his data pad, tapping the screen a few times. "Tell you what, kids, you can have the honeymoon suite at no extra charge. It's got a shower built for two *and* a king-sized bed."

We had a lot better than that at home, but we hadn't been home in a while. After sixteen days with the minuscule shower and bed on the spaceship, the honeymoon suite sounded downright luxurious. We both thanked the clerk profusely and let him show us to the room. We spent a few minutes laughing and rolling back and forth on the bed, enjoying all the room we had on it. Then we took our first long, slow shower in sixteen days. The effectively endless supply of warm water was like heaven to us. And while we had a larger shower at home, it turned out this one was plenty large enough for everything we wanted to do.

Clean, refreshed, and with one hunger sated, we headed out to satisfy our other hunger. The clerk suggested a couple of good restaurants which served local food. The one we chose had just the right combination of familiar and exotic tastes. After days of our own cooking, we reveled in the meal and left a nice tip.

Getting into the car, Michelle said, "Let's drive around for a while. The weather is nice and I'm not in a hurry to surround myself with walls again so soon."

"Far be it from me to refuse the request of a pretty girl," I said. "Fortunately, my wife doesn't expect me back at any particular time."

We'd been driving around for about half an hour when we saw the sign pointing the way to the Terran Federation office park. Without giving it a second thought, I followed the signs. We decided this was as good a time as any to get the lay of the land around the Psi Corps office. Only, when we reached the office park there was no sign of Psi Corps anywhere.

"Where else would they put it?" Michelle asked.

"Search me. I guess we could request a map," I said, tapping the map control on the dashboard.

Michelle quickly grabbed my hand, stopping me from doing anything else. "That's a bad idea, babe. Do you really want the local traffic system to have a record of a request for directions to Psi Corps just a day or two before a psychic evaluation machine is stolen?"

I smacked myself on the forehead. "No, of course not. How could I be so stupid?"

Michelle rubbed a hand up and down my arm. "In your entire life, the only time you've had to think like a fugitive was when we went off to rescue your parents. It's not surprising you're not back in that mindset yet."

"You managed to slide into it easily enough."

"Yeah, but Daddy's been teaching me this stuff for half my life," Michelle said. "I'm *supposed* to think this way. And mentioning thinking a certain way, drive around the buildings. If we can find a listing of the various offices, maybe it will point the way to Psi Corps."

We found a handy directory with arrows pointing the way to the various offices. And right at the bottom, in print so small Michelle had to get out of the car to read it, was a paragraph giving directions to the Psi Corps facility.

Sliding back into the car, Michelle said, "Maybe this place was already full when Psi Corps decided to put an office on Wolf. Anyway, I've got the directions."

We drove for another ten minutes before turning onto a long stretch of road. In our headlights, the area looked desolate, without a building in sight. We drove for what seemed like forever, though it was really only about eight kilometers. We didn't see any cars, but we did finally spot the lights of a facility ahead of us. As we drew closer, we realized the road ended at the entrance to Psi Corps—an entrance guarded by half a dozen armed men.

"Should I turn around here?" I asked.

"That would look too suspicious," Michelle responded. "Let's just drive down there and play the bewildered, lost tourists."

"And hope someone on Draconis hasn't gotten our photos out to all of the Psi Corps offices," I added.

"Yeah, that too," Michelle murmured.

With my heart hammering in my chest, I decelerated as we drew near the guard post. When we were twenty meters away, two of the guards raised their guns and took aim.

A guard stepped out in front of the car, his hand raised. I came to a stop as another guard approached the window. I lowered it, trying to put a clueless smile in place.

"This is a restricted facility," he said. "What's your business here?"

"Um, nothing?" I replied. "We were looking for..."

The guard's eyes narrowed as I trailed off without any actual explanation. Then Michelle leaned across and smiled up at the man.

"We're sorry, sir. We were just driving around looking for an out of the way spot under the stars." Michelle waved a hand as if trying to find the right words to say. "A place to...you know."

The guard's eyebrows drew down and I heard one of the others mutter, "Lucky bastard."

Michelle looked down as if too embarrassed to meet the guard's gaze. "We've been in a tiny spaceship cabin for ages and... um...I guess we just took the wrong road?"

"I'm going to need to see your IDs," the guard said, his tone all business. As we fumbled for them, he turned hard eyes on me. "Young man, Wolf isn't like the rest of the Federation. If you impregnate this young woman, you *will* be required to marry her."

Handing our identification cards to him, I cracked a smile. "What, again?"

This time the guard's eyebrows rose high and he studied the cards I'd handed to him. Then he passed them to one of the other guards. "Check 'em and log 'em."

While the second guard did as he was instructed, our formerly-gruff guard leaned down and actually smiled at Michelle. To my surprise, his face didn't break. "Assuming everything checks out and you two still want to do it under the stars, get your car to map the way to Cub Lake. There's plenty of nice, private spots out there."

The other guard returned and handed our identification cards to the man at our window. "Everything is in order, sir. They got married eight months ago on Draconis."

Handing the cards back to us, the man tipped his hat and said, "You two have a good night."

"Thank you, sir," I said, putting the car in reverse and backing into a turn in the wide entrance area. Seconds later, we were speeding down the highway back toward Pacrun. "Damn, damn, damn!"

"Yeah, now they've got a record of us at the facility," Michelle added glumly. "Besides, that place looks like some sort of fortress. There's no way we can go through with our original plan."

"What now?" I couldn't keep the bitterness out of my voice.

"We'll think of something, babe." Michelle leaned her head against my shoulder. "We'll think of something."

We drove the rest of the way back in silence. Once back in the city's urban area, I spotted what looked like a dive bar. I parked in the first free spot I found.

"Why are you stopping?" Michelle asked.

"I want a beer. Or maybe two or three," I said, still unable to keep my emotions under check. "We can celebrate having spent two weeks in that damned spaceship for nothing."

Michelle linked arms with me, but I kept my hands shoved in my pockets. I just didn't feel like being comforted at the moment.

"It wasn't all for nothing," she said. "We did get away from Psi Corps on Draconis and it's a safe bet they have no idea where we are right now."

"Yeah, whatever," I muttered, throwing open the door to the bar.

If possible, the bar looked worse inside than it did on the outside. The place was about half-full of rough and insular-looking people, the kind who generally don't take well to strangers. Most of the crowd looked like older versions of the gang who chased me off the train and into Michelle's arms all those months ago.

Michelle tugged at my arm. "I don't like the looks of this place, babe. Let's just grab some beer at a store and take it back to our hotel."

Over the last few months, one thing I have learned to do with my empathic ability is keep it in what I call 'scanner' mode. It lets me gauge the emotional mood of people around us. What I was getting from this crowd wasn't reassuring. There were a bunch of predators in there and showing fear before them was the wrong thing to do. If we backed away now, they'd come after us. We were well equipped to defend ourselves, but street security cams would catch everything and send police to investigate. And if Psi Corps *had* gotten out an alert for us...

Pulling Michelle inside, I quietly said, "If we leave now, we're going to have to fight out in the streets."

Michelle sighed, "And we can't risk police involvement. I don't like it, but I get it."

We went to the bar and ordered a couple of beers. A lot of eyes tracked us as we made our way to a table against one of the walls. Sitting down, I took a sip of the beer and, hard though I tried, couldn't keep from making a face.

"That bad?" Michelle turned her head and faced me though her eyes continued sweeping the bar for signs of trouble.

"Worse," I replied.

Out of the corner of my eye, I saw a couple get up and saunter our way. They were only a few years older than us and the man had his arm resting on the woman's shoulder in a possessive manner. I didn't need my ability to read their menace, but I used it anyway.

Leaning toward Michelle, I whispered, "Best guess is they're checking to see if we're going to be easy marks."

The couple stopped next to our table and just stood there staring at us. I leaned back, looped an arm over the back of my chair, and stared back. Michelle ignored them and took a sip of her beer. Shuddering, she put her mug down and pushed it away.

"You don't like our beer?" the man demanded.

The woman smirked. "She be one of them delicate types, hon. I bet she ain't never tasted beer afore."

"If so, she *still* hasn't tasted beer," I drawled. The pair scrunched their faces up, not following my line of reasoning. I helpfully added, "Because this is more like horse piss than beer."

"That's my favorite beer yer slammin', boy," he growled.

The woman was far from the sharpest knife in the drawer, but she was sharper than her companion. "Hey, was you mocking us?"

Talk in the bar died down as everyone watched the little drama playing out at our table. I broadened my scan to include everyone in the bar. To my complete lack of surprise, Michelle and I didn't have anyone on our side in here. I read increasing hostility and, in the back of my mind, knew I should search for some way to calm down the situation. Instead, the crowd's reaction just fed my bitterness over the trip out to Psi Corps and my long simmering anger over everything that had happened to us since that dinner with Jonas and Magda.

I suddenly found myself on my feet, glaring at the couple. "Yes, I am mocking you."

"You gonna let him get away with that, hon?" the woman asked.

"Naw, I sure ain't."

Michelle stood up. "There's no need for a fight. Why don't I buy you guys a beer and then we'll just leave you to drink in peace."

"Aw, ain't that cute, hon," the woman sneered. "She don't want you to hurt her little man."

"Too bad, blondie. I'm gonna hurt him real bad," the man sneered as the woman reached over to shove Michelle out of the way.

Michelle grabbed the woman's arm, twisted it until she yelped in pain, and then shoved her into her man. The two tangled and fell to the floor. I felt the anger build in them as they got back up. The man yelled something to the others in the bar. I couldn't understand a word he said because I had something building inside of me, too.

It was strange, something I'd never felt before, and it focused my empathic abilities like nothing I'd ever experienced. I easily felt the anger spiking in the patrons, picked up the building fear in a few of the hangers-on, and the resignation from the bar owner that his place was going to get trashed again.

The woman drew a switchblade and slashed at Michelle. My

wife blocked the clumsy attack, knocked the knife out of the woman's hand, and elbowed her in the gut. The woman dropped to the floor, gasping for the wind Michelle knocked out of her. That's when the man drew a gun and everything changed.

Whatever had been building inside of me burst free. Somehow, I pulled all of the anger out of everyone in that bar. One second, they were all ready to kill us. The next second they were completely devoid of anger. The shift was so sudden, some of them collapsed. The man who challenged us lowered his gun in confusion, falling back a few steps. Only Michelle, who wasn't angry, was unaffected.

The thing is all of that anger had to go somewhere. As it drained from everyone in the bar, it flowed into me. Anger became rage became wrath became cold, implacable fury.

I stalked toward the man and whatever expression I wore terrified him. The blood drained from his face and he stumbled back from my advance. He caught his foot on a chair and fell, the gun clattering from his hand. I squatted down next to him and the man curled up into a quivering ball. I picked up the gun and examined it idly.

"So you're going to hurt me 'real bad,' are you?" My voice was so cold I half-expected frost to form in the man's hair.

The man shook his head violently and a wet stain spread over his groin.

"How nice that you don't want to hurt me anymore," I said. "Too bad I don't feel the same way about you."

All around me, stunned people watched in silence as I carefully placed the gun against the man's head. I held it there, basking in the fury inside me and the growing fear around me.

I reveled in the furious bliss for a few seconds then leaned over the man and gently whispered, "It's time to die, little man."

I felt a sharp pain in my wrist and the gun fell from my hand, stopping me from killing the mewling little man quivering before me. My head snapped up and I saw a blonde woman standing over me. I gave into the white hot fury coursing through me and rose quickly. Before she could react, my left hand snapped out and grabbed the blonde around the throat.

"You ruined my shot," I snarled.

The woman clawed at my hand futilely, her strength no match for mine. I tightened my grip, watching her face turn red. Grinning in anticipation, I balled my right hand into a fist, preparing to pummel her face to a bloody pulp.

Movement at my feet drew my attention away from the blonde though I didn't release my grip. Quivering boy was slowly reaching for the gun the blonde had kicked from my hand. I raised my foot and stomped hard on his fingers. I felt bones break under my heel and thrilled to the scream of agony the man made.

Wagging a finger at him, I said, "Uh uh, no gun for you. Just lay there for a minute until I finish with blondie, okay?"

I turned back to the woman who continued prying at the hand around her throat. Finding her strength insufficient, she suddenly raked her fingernails down the back of my hand and then sank them into my arm. Pain caused me to release my grip and she stumbled back from me, drawing deep breaths as she went.

I found myself torn between pursuing the woman who hurt me and shooting the man who irritated me so badly. In that second of indecision, the woman spoke.

"Matt, this isn't you! I don't know what happened, but the man I married wouldn't do any of this."

How did she know my name? And what did she mean by 'married'? Confusion gave me further pause, and from the far away deep back part of my brain, a memory cut through the fury. Michelle. The blonde was Michelle. The woman I'd loved forever. And I'd tried to kill her.

Then the fury welled up again. So what if I tried to kill the little bitch. She stopped me from finishing off the idiot at my feet. She *hurt* me! She deserved whatever happened to her.

No! No no no no no! By all that is holy, *no*! I felt the fury slip, lose some of its control over me. I kept fighting it, pushing and clawing my way out of the deep recesses of my mind, struggling to save myself and my wife.

"Michelle," I croaked, "I'm losing it. Get me out of here."

Without another word, Michelle grabbed my arm and all but dragged me toward the door. No one moved to stop us.

"Hurry. I don't know what will happen when the anger leaves me," I pleaded.

She shoved open the door and led me out. As soon as we were on the street, she burst into a run, pulling me toward our car. Halfway there, I lost it—the anger flowed away from me as quickly as it had come. With a sick feeling in my stomach, I realized the anger was returning to its source. We had bare seconds before the bar patrons came after us.

"It's gone, Michelle," I gasped. "Back to the people in the bar."

As if in answer, a howl rose from inside the bar and, a couple of seconds later, the door burst open and men piled out. One pointed our way. "There they are!"

With shouts of rage, the mob from the bar ran after us. We reached the car and Michelle shoved me in before diving into the driver's seat. She punched the starter and the car hummed to life. Then Michelle stomped on the accelerator and sped down the road.

A gunshot sounded, followed by another. Michelle spun the wheel and turned down the first side street she came to. With buildings between the mob and us, the gunfire was no longer a worry. She still kept the car floored, weaving in and out of the sparse nighttime traffic with practiced ease.

"What the hell happened back there, Matt?" she asked, concern evident in her voice even as her concentration never left the road.

"I don't know, exactly," I replied. "I mean I know *what* happened, just not really *how* it happened. Something built up inside of me and when that guy threatened us it just burst out and I...I guess absorbed is as good a word as any. I absorbed all of the anger in the room. Every last bit of it drained out of the people in the bar and into me."

"God above, babe. Are you okay?" Michelle asked.

"Yeah. I guess. The rage just took over and made me into a cold, calculating psycho killer or something." My voice shook as I related what happened. I felt a shiver run up my spine when I thought about what *could* have happened. "I didn't kill anyone— which is probably some kind of miracle... I didn't hurt you, did I?"

Unconsciously, Michelle brought a hand to her throat, which was only now returning to its normal color. "It wasn't fun, that's for sure. But you didn't do anything permanent. Even when I was trying to draw a full breath, I was more worried about you than I was about me."

"What do we do now?" I asked.

"We get off of this planet right now," Michelle answered. "Once those people take the time to think about what happened, someone is bound to think of calling Psi Corps. The reward for finding rogue psychics is big enough that they may choose to call them before calling the cops."

"Great. Looks like I've ruined things for us here. Less than ten hours on planet and I've already forced us to dump a set of IDs and a ship transponder."

"Hey, don't think about it like that, Matt," Michelle said, rubbing my leg gently. "Maybe you should think of it as a major breakthrough with your power."

"Yeah, I'm sure there's going to be a big call for furious psychopaths all around the Federation," I said, my tone once again bitter. "I could set up my own crowd control business and make a fortune absorbing the anger from riots. It'll be worth it as long as I can keep myself from killing more than five or six people, right?"

"That's *not* what I meant. Take a minute and think this through. What were you feeling before you absorbed all the anger? It was something strong, wasn't it? And you have powerful emotions when we're making love, too. So maybe we've found the first part of the puzzle to your ability."

In the distance, I heard a siren, then a second. And a third. "I guess the guys at the bar called the police. Or the bar owner did, anyway."

"Don't sweat it. We'll reach the spaceport long before the cops can catch us. But I guess I should concentrate on my driving and you should get your mind back in order." Michelle patted my arm. "We're going to need to take off as fast as possible once we get to the ship. Can you handle that?"

"Of course. I like to think I'm at my best when you're depending on me to get us out of trouble." I cracked a smile, though I didn't feel at all like smiling at the moment.

The car rocketed up the hill from the city and onto the spaceport plateau. Far behind us, flashing lights broke free of the city and raced after us. Michelle was right, there was no way they'd catch us before we reached the spaceship. Jonas and Dad also carefully selected a ship with a fast startup time and a special streamlined startup for real emergencies. This definitely counted as a real emergency.

Then we got our first look at the spaceport gate. Port security had a roadblock set up across it.

"Hang on, babe," Michelle said, aiming for the closest thing to a gap in the roadblock. "The ride is about to get real bumpy."

I looked at the size of the vehicles blocking the gate—they were a *lot* bigger than our rental car. Too bad this was an all ground-car planet because a repulser hop would come in real handy right about now.

"Are you sure you can punch through that gap?" I asked, my voice rising as I braced myself for impact.

"Not a chance," Michelle said, her voice as calm as could be. "But those security guys don't know that I know that."

"Uh, what does that—?"

Michelle interrupted my question with a sharp turn to the left. The rear end of the car swung around and scraped the fender of one of the security trucks. People dove every which a way, trying to get clear of the impact they thought was coming. Instead,

Michelle swung us onto an access road running around the outside of the fence.

"Can we just crash through the fence somewhere away from the gate?" I asked once I got my breath back.

"Nope. The fence is just the visual barrier," Michelle responded. "If you look closely, you'll see the whole thing is glowing slightly."

I looked closely. Then looked again before finally seeing it. A ten-foot high forcefield ran around the spaceport, providing far better security than any metal fence ever could.

"How on earth did you see that while driving?" I asked. "I can barely see the glow right now and I'm looking for it."

"I noticed it on the way out of the spaceport earlier today," Michelle said. "You were giving the guard our IDs and I had plenty of time to look around."

"And you just thought it would be a good time to study the security layout?" It was a rhetorical question. Of course, Michelle studied the layout. Her father spent most of her life drilling that into her. She could probably stop breathing more easily than she could stop looking for possible threats.

"Okay, what's the plan now?" I asked. "Is there some place we can ram the fence without wrecking the car? Or maybe a ramp or something you're going to use to jump the fence?"

"This isn't one of your adventure vids, Matt," Michelle replied, laughter bubbling up in her tone. Was that humorous laughter or just-short-of-hysterical laughter? "When we get close to our ship, I'm going to stop the car next to the fence. We'll climb up on the roof and jump over from there. We both have enough gymnastics training to do that."

"That's reasonable. Will we have time with all the pursuit that's coming after us?"

"I hope so. Mentioning pursuit, can you look back and tell me what the security guys are doing, babe?"

I turned around and looked toward the gate. The police cars weren't here, yet, but the security forces were mobilizing quickly.

"It looks like they've split up. Half are following us on this road and half are chasing us from inside the fence."

Michelle sighed. "That's the best I could have hoped for, I suppose. This would be a lot easier to pull off if they were all out here on the access road. Okay, time to look the other way. Can you see our ship?"

I gazed off into the distance, looking through the rows of parked spacecraft. Fortunately, Wolf isn't a high traffic planet, especially for small, personal ships like ours. "Yeah, it's about a kilometer away from us—at least the closest part of the fence to the ship is that far away."

"Got it. When we stop, get on top of the car, boost me over, and then jump over yourself."

"Good idea," I replied. I had always been better than Michelle at vertical leaps and was also a lot stronger than her. I could boost her over the fence easily enough and then clear it on my own. "Don't wait for me when you hit the ground. Take off for the ship. I'll catch up."

"You'd better," Michelle muttered. "Grab onto something, I'm stopping now."

"What? But you're still going full—"

Michelle suddenly cut the steering wheel to the right and jammed the brakes all the way to the floor. The car went into a tight spin before slamming into the force field and coming to a sudden stop.

I really just wanted to sit there and take a minute to get my bearings, but we didn't have anything close to a minute. Throwing my door open, I hopped out of the car and clambered onto the roof. I leaned back against the forcefield, feeling the tingle of energy along my back, and cupped my hands. Michelle swung onto the roof and immediately stepped into my cupped hands. As soon as her hands braced against my shoulders, I lifted her up over my head.

Then Michelle called, "Clear!"

I backed as far from the fence as I could—all of two steps—as she took off sprinting for the ship. I took one step, bounded into the air, planted my other foot against the force field, and pushed up again. I didn't clear the fence. Fortunately, I had no time to think about what came next. I wrapped my hands over the barbed top of the fence, which stuck out from the forcefield, and swung myself over.

Sharp metal ripped into the palms of my hands and blood flowed freely. Ignoring the pain, I concentrated on my landing. A twisted ankle, like the one I got months ago when the gang of thugs chased me off the train, would be a real disaster now. I tucked and rolled as I hit the ground, then came up running.

Michelle was already twenty meters away and running at top speed. I sprinted after her, taking a look to my right to check on the approaching security forces. They were still half a kilometer away and were slowed by the parked spaceships they had to drive around.

I was feeling pretty good about our chances until the first blaster bolt ricocheted off the tarmac ahead of me. Then the air seemed as if it was filled with blaster fire. It was probably only half a dozen men firing at me—from moving, swerving vehicles, no less —but it damn sure seemed like a lot of people were taking pot shots at me.

I found myself dodging, cutting left and right, and generally acting like some kind of stunt man in an action vid. Michelle looked over her shoulder, her eyes widening at the sight behind her. I was afraid she'd turn and come to help. Instead, she put on an extra burst of speed and dove through the spaceship's airlock. I kept dodging and twisting and generally doing my best to make myself a hard target to hit. Several of the shots came far too close, including one that splashed pieces of tarmac up against my legs.

Didn't these guys know that Psi Corps wanted me alive?

Then the unthinkable happened. I planted a foot to cut to the left and it came down in a divot dug out of the tarmac by one of the earlier blaster shots. My foot slipped out from under me and I went down hard on my left side. My ribs screamed in protest and some of my breath was driven out in a whoosh. Then my head bounced off the tarmac and bright lights burst open before my eyes.

I struggled to stand up. I struggled to breathe. I struggled to stop my head from spinning. And I struggled to see beyond the private light show going on in my head. When it all cleared enough for me to stand, I found my balance was iffy at best. I spun in a slow circle, trying to find our spaceship. When I spotted it, I tried running toward it. The best I could manage was a stumbling shamble and even that tended to veer to the left. I had to stop and reorient myself on the spaceship every few steps.

And then something came between me and the spaceship. I stopped, trying to figure out if I'd gone off course again, but I still saw the familiar nose of the ship poking up from the thing blocking my way.

I concentrated on the thing and it refused to come into focus. I shook my head in an attempt to clear my vision. Bad idea. *Very* bad idea. Stars blew up in my head again and pain shot through it. From far away, I got the idea someone was shouting something, but I couldn't understand what they were saying. Hell, I didn't even know if they were shouting at me. Little shapes moved all around the bigger shape that was in my way. Somewhere in the back of my brain, I figured those were the security people. They probably weren't happy with me and Michelle right now.

Michelle. Where was she? Oh, yeah, *she* got to the spaceship. She was safe. At least she could get away from here. Besides, what would Psi Corps want with her? She's not the psychic. I waited for the ship to lift off and take my wife to safety. It didn't happen.

Instead, something moved on the skin of the spaceship. I figured it was my head playing tricks on me since it looked like the ship's skin was moving around. And then long things poked out of the ship and there was more flashing. All those little things—the security people—scattered as the big thing just sort of melted.

A booming, beautiful voice filled the area and shook my entire body. I even sort of understood what it said.

"Back away from the man and you will not be harmed. As long as he walks unmolested into this spaceship, everyone gets out of this alive." The voice paused for a moment, before continuing. "Okay, babe, they're backing off. You need to come to the ship."

I stood there for a few seconds before remembering *I* was the one she was calling 'babe.' Smiling at that thought, I slowly walked around the big, melty thing. A few of the small things—security guys, I really need to remember they're security guys not 'things'—stood well off to the side watching me. I gave them a smile and a little wave and then stumbled into the spaceship.

The airlock door closed behind me and then Michelle was at my side, guiding me to a seat at the controls. "Do you think you can fly the ship, Matt?"

Through force of will, I tried to make the controls stop spinning and failed miserably. "Ummmm, nope."

"That's just fan-damn-tastic," she muttered, punching a few buttons on the controls.

While lights blinked and other stuff whirred, Michelle grabbed a first aid kit from the wall brackets. She rolled up my sleeve and slapped a med unit onto my arm. As my arm prickled from the unit's probes, Michelle plopped down in the pilot's seat.

She took a few seconds to check the exterior cams, grimaced, then fired off a few laser blasts. Leaning toward a microphone, she said, "Stand back or else. We're lifting off now."

Michelle turned off the mic and looked at me. "*Please* be a minor injury that's easy to fix. I've got a bad feeling that we're going to need a real pilot soon." Turning back to the controls, she said, "Autopilot, liftoff."

"Systems startup incomplete," a soothing voice replied.

"Emergency override zeta three seven," Michelle said.

"Emergency override activated," the voice said. "Liftoff in five, four, three, two, one."

The engines roared and our spaceship rose into the night sky.

# WE CAN'T CATCH A BREAK

O ur ship accelerated away from Wolf in a graceful upward arc. I, on the other hand, was a lot less graceful, bending over the side of the co-pilot's chair and puking my guts out. I found myself wishing Michelle and I never got around to dinner.

A beep sounded from my arm and a mechanical voice said, "Diagnostic complete. The patient has a concussion."

"That explains a lot," Michelle said. "Med unit, can you correct the concussion?"

"Yes, though it is not recommended. The patient will recover naturally with rest," the unit responded. "Nanite intervention is only advisable if the patient hasn't the time to heal naturally."

"Oh, lovely. Rest. Relaxation. Yes, we're going to have *lots* of time for that." Michelle sounded upset, but I couldn't quite get my brain to remember why.

"Don't worry, hon," I said, tapping my head. That hurt, but I grinned anyway. "I've got a really hard head. It'll be okay."

"Your head might be okay, but what about the patrol ships in orbit around Wolf?" Michelle asked. "How are we going to get away from them without a pilot?"

"Oooooh. Now *that* is a good question," I replied. "Can I get back to you on it?"

Then we cleared the atmosphere and the comm light began blinking. Without giving it a second thought—or maybe even a first thought—I answered the comm.

"Yello. Or maybe green. I can never choose." I considered the options for a second and then said, "Maybe you can choose for me?"

"Who is this?" a harsh, female voice demanded.

"Don't you know?" I asked. "You called me."

"Look, I don't know what you think you're—"

"It would be polite for *you* to introduce yourself, first," I interrupted and then continued in a sing-song voice, "I will if you will."

"Fine, we'll play your stupid game. This is Captain Carol Odenton, commanding the Wolf Planetary Defense Force Gunship Alpha. Who—"

I burst out laughing. "Oh, oh! I get it—you're on the alpha of the Wolf navy. That's pretty funny."

"Is there someone who is not an idiot I can talk to? We are in pursuit and are authorized to use force to keep you from leaving the system."

I considered that for a minute. "Do you mean that Wolf is such a crappy place to live you have to *force* people to stay here? That's just wrong, Captain Lady."

At this point, Michelle interrupted and took over the conversation. I was glad to let her do it. This captain wasn't making *any* sense at all.

"Captain Odenton, my husband has a concussion. There is *no* disrespect intended."

"Uh huh. We'll have our doctor check him out—right after you reverse thrust and hold position for boarding."

Wow, the captain really was bossy. I opened my mouth to tell her that, but Michelle covered it with her hand. Never let it be said I can't take a hint. I licked her palm.

"What are the grounds for your demand, Captain Odenton?"

Michelle said, remaining much too polite for my tastes. "We've done nothing wrong."

"According to my sources, you fled a crime scene–"

"Of course we fled the crime scene, Captain! *We* were the intended victims of the crime," Michelle snarled.

The bossy captain showed she was rude, too, raising her voice and talking over Michelle. "Then you broke into the shipyard, slagged a security vehicle, shot at security personnel, and lifted off without clearance." The captain's voice sounded smug. "I have *plenty* of grounds for my demand. Accede to it or I will be forced to fire on your engines and disable you. We will do our best to minimize damage to the rest of the ship, but I cannot guarantee the safety of anyone on board."

Michelle grimaced. "Autopilot, can we outrun the patrol ship?"

"Don't be foolish, girl," the bossy captain said. "You're not going to get away from us."

At the same time, the calm voice of the autopilot responded, "This ship has superior acceleration, but the patrol ship has superior maximum thrust. Given sufficient time, the patrol ship will surpass this ship's velocity and catch this ship."

Michelle's shoulders slumped and I really wished there was something I could do to make her feel better. But she needed a good pilot and here I sat, all messed up in the head. If only there was a way to fix my head. Then I remembered there *was* a way.

"Med unit," I said, "please fix me up as good as new."

Michelle spun to face me. "Babe, no! The med unit said it was better if you just rested."

"Your instructions are unclear," the med unit chirped. "Do you wish nanite intervention for your concussion?"

"Yes," I said.

"No!" Michelle said a second later.

"Commencing nanite intervention," the med unit said.

I grinned at Michelle. "Beat you to it."

Michelle closed her eyes and whispered, "God, please don't let my husband die."

"I most definitely do not want anyone to die," the gunship captain said, not having figured out Michelle wasn't talking to her. "All you have to do is reverse your thrusters and I promise you won't be harmed."

"Autopilot, set a course for wormhole epsilon. Execute at full acceleration," Michelle said.

"Acknowledged. Proceeding at full acceleration," the autopilot responded.

The subtle hum of the engines increased quickly as the autopilot brought us up to full thrust. I wasn't surprised when the irritating captain voiced her disapproval.

"That was not a smart decision, girl," the captain growled. "I hope you live to regret it."

"Oh, shut up, woman," Michelle snapped. "The only laws my husband and I have broken are ones governments—both local and Federal—have forced us to break. All my husband and I want to do is live our lives in peace—only people like you won't let us."

With a click, Michelle muted the comm channel and sat back. "Autopilot, how long will it take us to reach wormhole epsilon and how long before the patrol ship is in firing range?"

"Nine minutes, sixteen seconds to the wormhole," the autopilot said, "and seven minutes, two seconds until the patrol ship is within firing range."

Michelle leaned back in her chair, rubbing her temples. "Med unit, how long does the concussion repair take?"

"The patient will be fully functional in six minutes, three seconds."

I pumped my fist in the air. "Woo hoo! The med unit wins."

Michelle stood up. "Matt, why don't you move to the pilot's seat? We won't have much time to spare once the nanites finish working on you."

"Righto, Commander Comely," I said. I'd hoped for a laugh from Michelle, but I guess she wasn't in a laughing mood. Standing carefully—my head still felt strange, after all—I kissed Michelle lovingly. "Don't worry, hon. I'm sure I'll think of something once I can think again."

Michelle guided me into the other chair. "I'm sure you will, babe, but right now you'd better sit down before you fall down."

After I was seated, Michelle leaned over the back of the chair and wrapped her arms around me. Resting her chin on my shoulder, she said, "Med unit, alert us when there are fifteen seconds left before the concussion repairs are completed."

"Acknowledged," the unit said.

Michelle stayed right there with me as nanites worked on my brain and the patrol ship drew inexorably closer. When the med unit gave the fifteen second warning, she kissed my cheek and whispered, "I love you, Matt."

"I love you, too, Michelle," I said as she released me and took her seat at the communications and weapons control board.

Then my mind cleared and I leaned over the pilot's controls. "Autopilot, disengage but continue tracking the patrol ship. Alert me when it's in firing range." The controls unlocked and I ran my fingers over them, entering commands. "Michelle, on my mark, deploy three decoys. I'm sending courses to your board now."

Not wasting any time asking about my plan, Michelle quickly did as I asked. "Decoys ready."

Time slowed to a crawl as the last few seconds ticked by. Finally, the autopilot announced, "The patrol ship is in range."

A second later, Michelle said, "Missiles launched."

I heard the nervous tension in Michelle's voice as she announced the missile launches. "So much for just trying to hit the engines," she added.

"Yeah, well, they probably got carried away in the excitement of the chase," I said, giving them more credit than the captain deserved. "They still aren't in range for lasers, so maybe she's hoping we'll give up. Then she can just disarm the missiles."

"Right, babe, but you've got your brilliant plan that's going to take care of those missiles, right?"

"Of course, hon. We haven't even celebrated our first

anniversary yet, so I'm not going to let us get blown to bits." I turned a bright smile on Michelle, hoping for a disarming effect.

It worked. She returned my smile with a devilish one of her own. "Admit it, you just want to see what I'm going to give you for an anniversary present."

"You're getting me something? Aw, that's so sweet," I bantered back. "Can you give me a hint? Is it a new sports flier?"

"I'll never tell—but it's really more of an activity than an actual thing," Michelle replied, turning back to her controls.

"Oh, an *activity* sounds like fun," I said. "Please tell me it involves getting naked."

"How about I tell you the missiles have closed half the distance between us and the patrol ship, instead?" Michelle asked. "Is it time to implement your plan?"

"Almost. I want them to get closer so the missiles have a better chance of locking on the decoys when we launch them. Mentioning the decoys, we're launching the first two on my mark. Hold the third until after my course correction."

"We're changing courses? How nice of you to tell me," Michelle growled.

"Sorry, you distracted me with all that talk about naked activities."

"*I* said activities, *you* added the naked part," Michelle said with a short laugh.

"Yes, we're changing course. There's no way we can reach wormhole epsilon before the patrol ship gets well within laser range. They'll definitely be able to take out our engines then." I brought up a chart with my new course. "So we're going to change course for wormhole delta and hope the missiles bite on the decoys."

"Do we have any idea where wormhole delta goes?" Michelle asked. "Epsilon goes to a fairly big colony out beyond the Federation border."

"All I had time to check was that delta went to a system with a second wormhole," I replied. "It wouldn't do to just head off into an interstellar cul-de-sac."

"And what about the patrol ship?"

"We're a lot more maneuverable than it," I said. "We can make a pretty tight course correction. The patrol ship will have to swing much wider than us. They'll never get close enough for lasers before we enter wormhole delta."

"If you say so, pilot dear." Michelle checked her missile track again. "Is it time to launch the decoys yet? Those things are getting way too close for comfort."

"Almost," I said, watching the missiles close on us. "Prepare for decoy launch on my mark... *Now!*"

Michelle punched two buttons simultaneously and a metallic thump sounded through the ship. "Decoys one and two are away... They're broadcasting our signal and are breaking off on their own course...One missile bit."

"What about the second decoy? Did anything follow it?"

"No," Michelle shook her head. "We've still got two missiles on our tail. Can we outrun them?"

"I wish," I said. "That's what the third decoy is for."

I ran my hands over the pilot's controls and the ship rotated away from our direct course to wormhole epsilon. "Get ready to launch the third drone."

I watched the ship's heading swinging around toward the course I'd laid in for the other wormhole. Halfway through the course change, I said, "Launch the decoy."

A final thump resounded in the ship as the miniature rocket sped away from us. Michelle and I watched the track of the two remaining missiles, waiting for them to show their course—and, of course, only one of the missiles locked on the drone. Without any more decoys prepped for launch, I prepared for evasive maneuvers. At the same time, Michelle leaned over her weapons console and deployed several lasers.

About then, the comm burst to life as the annoying patrol ship captain contacted us. "Nice try, kids, but you're not going to get away that easily. Come about to an intercept course with us and I'll send a self-destruct order to the missile."

"You know, she's starting to get on my nerves. I should have turned the comm off instead of just muting it on our end," Michelle said. Her fingers punched buttons and the display showed laser shots lancing out at the approaching missile. The first few shots missed by a wide margin, but Michelle quickly narrowed her aim, firing port and starboard laser batteries in sequence and retargeting after each shot.

"Do you think you can hit the missile?" I asked.

"The missiles are designed so targeting systems have trouble getting a lock on them. Even so, if I had another minute, I would definitely get it," she said. "But we've got about half that time before it catches us, so I really don't know. It all depends on what the captain does at this point."

"Huh?"

"If she gets worried that my shots are coming too close, she'll tell the missile to go into an evasion pattern," Michelle said.

"Won't that make it harder to hit the missile?"

"You'd think so," Michelle said, "but it's not very useful against someone trained in missile defense. If I setup a criss-crossing pattern of rapid shots from the lasers, there's a good chance the missile will wander into the firing line."

"That's...counter-intuitive," I said.

"You get a lot of that with automated weapons systems. The missile can't carry an AI because an AI can develop a sense of self-preservation. If it does, the AI will save itself by veering off course entirely." While talking to me, Michelle kept firing, her eyes glued on the missile track. "The best a missile can carry is a programmed random course generator. The thing is it still has to stay so close to its original course that even a random course change can't be very random. If there are multiple missiles or if the gunner is untrained, random evasion procedures can work well. Thanks to your decoys, we've only got one missile. And, well, you know how Daddy is—he made sure I was trained."

Something changed on her display and Michelle suddenly barked a triumphant, "Yes!"

She hit a key and then sat back. "There's nothing else we can do now, Matt. Just keep your fingers crossed..."

The missile track suddenly flashed and winked out. Michelle pumped a fist in the air. "She shoots, she scores!"

Michelle propped an elbow on her console and leaned her head against her hand. Blue eyes shining, she said, "You're all clear, babe. Let's get out of this system."

"I think your celebration is a little premature, hon," I replied. "They've launched another three missiles."

"You'll reach the wormhole before the missiles can catch us," Michelle said, not even bothering to check the tracking system. "The missiles will lose their lock during the wormhole transit. All we have to do is run dark when we come out the other side. When the missiles exit, we just wait until the missiles run out of fuel or lock onto something else."

A few minutes later, with our ship still well ahead of the cluster of missiles, we entered the wormhole and left Federation space behind us.

Our trip through the wormhole was going to take four hours. I had all sorts of ideas for how to pass the time. Michelle had other ideas, insisting on hooking me up to the full-sized med unit in the ship's tiny sickbay for a full checkup. My protests that the portable med unit fixed me up just fine fell on deaf ears.

"God above, Matt, what is it with men and medicine?" Michelle demanded as she connected me to the unit. "Women take their health seriously and, fortunately for the entire medical profession's bottom line, take the health of their men seriously, too."

"Sorry, hon," I muttered, "I guess it's just the way we men are built."

"Then it's really lucky for you men that we women love you," she replied as she connected the last lead and sat back to wait for the exam results.

"While the unit runs its checks, why don't you find out as much about the star system we're heading for as possible?" I asked, changing the subject as far from sex-based medical attitudes as possible.

Michelle nodded, pulled her data pad out, and tapped on the screen for a few seconds. She read the information on the screen, frowning as she did so. Finally, Michelle said, "It's called the Pride system. Someone with a sense of humor probably named it to contrast with Wolf. But there's nothing in the system worth feeling pride over. It's a weak red star with a couple of planets much too far from the star to support life."

"What about an asteroid belt?"

"Yeah, there's a small one," Michelle replied. "I wouldn't call it a great place to hide, but if that Wolf patrol ship follows us through, it'll be better than nothing."

"What about the wormhole out of the system?"

"There are actually two, but one looks pretty useless. It goes to a star system so popular no one even named it. It's only got a numeric designation." Michelle tapped some keys on her controls. "The information we've got on it makes Pride look downright homey in comparison. The system is about as close as you can get to the ass-end of the universe. It's so useless that no one has bothered charting it for wormholes."

"Let's hope we don't have to run that way." I craned my neck trying to get a look at her screen. Michelle glared at me until I sat back. "What about the other wormhole?"

"Give me a sec..." Michelle punched a few keys and then she sighed. "It takes us back into Federation space—the Piscain Hub."

"Hm... As long as no one's looking for us, Piscain is a pretty good spot for us." The med unit beeped. Michelle handed her pad to me while she checked the medical report. I knew Piscain pretty well but skimmed the information just to be sure. "Piscain rivals Pegasus as a tourist destination, but it's got even more wormholes connecting to it—thirteen, overall."

"Do any of them head out of Federation space?" Michelle asked, most of her attention on the medical readout.

"No, but we'll only be a jump or two from the border," I responded. "Another bonus is the heavy traffic the hub gets. It actually makes Pegasus look like a little backwater way station. And the space station in the system is gigantic—something like eighty or ninety kilometers in diameter."

"All right, babe, the med report says you're fine. It still recommends some rest, but that's about it." She held out her hand for the data pad. She scanned the report herself as I finished removing medical leads. "You didn't mention the naval base in the system, Matt."

"Because you took the pad from me before I could. Since I know you can read as well as I can, it was kind of a moot point," I said.

"As long as it wasn't some misguided attempt to keep me from worrying my pretty little head over something we can't control."

In my most serious tone of voice, I said, "Do I look like a man who never wants to have sex again?"

Michelle burst out laughing. "I'm glad you understand how important it is for us to share everything—good and bad."

"You made that abundantly clear before we even got married." I grinned, "But mentioning sex..."

"Uh uh, Matt. You aren't getting into my pants until you've at least changed the ship's transponder to one of our other registration names. After that, we've got to figure out which wormhole to take away from Piscain."

"I'll have the transponder switched in no time. As for the Piscain decision, we're going to spend at least six hours in normal space traveling to the wormhole from Pride to Piscain. Then there's the three-and-a-half-hour wormhole transit time. That gives us nearly half a day to do research and make decisions—and that's after we exit this wormhole. We've still got nearly four hours left before that. I'm sure we can afford a *few* minutes for a little fun."

"It had better be a lot more than a few minutes, babe," Michelle said, looking up at me through lidded eyes. "Now get busy switching the transponder. I've got to prepare some messages for Daddy while you're doing that. We can send them as we pass through Piscain."

Michelle finished her work a lot sooner than I did and stopped by to check on my progress. "How much longer until you're finished with the transponder?"

"Maybe fifteen minutes?"

Smiling seductively, Michelle slowly unbuttoned her shirt and shrugged out of it. "Why don't you aim for ten?"

Spinning around, she walked away from me with an exaggerated swing to her hips. I finished with the transponder in eight minutes.

Considerably more than a few minutes later, Michelle propped herself on one elbow and absently brushed hair away from her face. Her eyes turned serious as she said, "Are you ready to talk about what happened in that bar back on Wolf?"

"Not really, but I know I've got to," I answered. "I don't really know how to describe what I did—it just came on me suddenly when that idiot and his girlfriend tried pushing us around. I was already upset about our trip out to the Psi Corps office—I *never* expected we'd find some kind of paramilitary facility."

"Me neither, Matt," Michelle said, laying her head on my chest. "On Draconis, Psi Corps just has a normal office downtown. Maybe it's different on the inside or maybe there's a maximum security Psi Corps facility hidden away somewhere on the planet..." Michelle absently stroked my cheek. "You know I'd never have suggested we go out there if—"

"Yes, Michelle, I know. That place surprised me as much as it did you." I kissed her lightly. "Did I ever compliment you on how well you handled those guards?"

"Don't change the subject, Matt," Michelle said. "You were describing what happened in the bar?"

I sighed theatrically. "That's the problem with smart women—

you can't distract them with compliments... So, I wasn't in the best of moods when the moron couple decided to pick on us."

Haltingly, I described how the odd feeling grew, how I just sucked all the anger out of the room, and how it overwhelmed me. Describing how the anger made me do those terrible things to Michelle, I wrapped my arms tightly around her. "Ever since we ran from that bar, I might have sounded like I was okay but I wasn't. I've been terrified that you wouldn't think of me the same way, anymore."

"You're an empath, Matt. Why didn't you just read me?"

"I tried, but my emotions were roiling too much. And then I got the concussion and then we were busy getting away from the patrol ship..." I ground to a halt, blinking away tears.

"And I was too busy concentrating on our getaway to realize what you were going through." A warm tear splashed on my chest. "I'm so sorry, babe. Is that why you were so desperate to get laid?"

"Not entirely, Michelle," I replied. "I mean, I'm always up for a roll in the hay with you."

Keeping her eyes on mine, Michelle's hand wandered down between my legs. Giggling, she said, "That much is obvious."

"All of my emotional knots just fell away when I felt the full force of your love flood into me," I said. "It was like I could breathe again."

Michelle straddled me and gently raked her fingernails down my chest. "There's only one way to make sure all of those emotional knots are gone—and I already know you're up for it."

*Much* later, Michelle asked, "How are you feeling now, babe?"

"Absolutely amazed that I'm married to a woman like you. And I'm a lot better."

"That's good, because we've got to prep for running dark after we exit the wormhole." Michelle rolled off of me and gathered her scattered clothes. "Just do me a favor and never, ever doubt my love again."

Pulling on my own clothes, I said, "I won't."

Half an hour later, we exited the wormhole and went dark. Two minutes after that, our passive sensors picked up the three missiles coming through. We kept an eye on the sensors, hoping they'd take off after some other target. We were still waiting when something else popped out of the wormhole and zipped past us on its way toward the wormhole to Piscain.

"What was that?" Michelle asked.

"A message drone," I replied, my tone flat. "It's a safe bet Piscain will know about us before we get there."

Watching the sensor screen as the message drone sped away, knowing we couldn't shoot at it or pursue it without attracting the attention of the three missiles, Michelle summed up my feelings in a single word. "Dammit."

Leaning back in my seat, I sighed, "Yeah. It's like we can't catch a break anymore."

"So, what do you think we ought to do, babe?" Michelle asked. "Take our chances with the patrol ship back in Wolf or a naval squadron in Piscain?"

"If I read Captain Odenton right, she's going to have a pretty heavy presence around wormhole delta for quite a while. She wasn't exactly happy with us and doesn't strike me as the forgiving sort."

"Yeah, me too," Michelle said. "We could surprise everyone by going to the unnamed system and looking for wormholes."

"No, we don't have the sensor suite necessary to actually detect a wormhole and the chances of us just stumbling into one are astronomically small," I replied. "And that's even assuming the system has more than one wormhole. Most don't."

"So, we go to the Piscain Hub and hope the navy isn't ready for us or isn't taking Odenton seriously?" Michelle shook her head. "That doesn't seem likely."

"I don't know," I said. "They probably don't watch the wormhole from this system very closely. It's not like there's going to be much traffic through it. If you check the various routes from the Piscain Hub, one of their other wormholes goes straight to Wolf. If we can get going soon, we might pop through before the navy mobilizes or, even better before they pick up the drone."

"Or Captain Odenton could have sent a second messenger drone through the direct route to Piscain and the navy will be ready for us," Michelle suggested in a dark tone.

"That won't give as much extra notice as you might think," I said. "Between the time required to reach that wormhole and the transit time in the wormhole, the theoretical second drone won't get there much more quickly than we will."

"Then maybe sending a second drone wasn't worth it for her."

"No, I think your first idea was right, hon," I replied. "It just makes good tactical sense to send a second drone. Odenton can't be sure we won't blow the first out to bits."

Michelle brightened suddenly. "Hey, one of those missiles locked onto something and is accelerating away from us."

"It's about time. How much fuel do you think the other two have, hon?"

"At their current thrust, maybe five minutes." Michelle glanced at me for a second. "How far behind the drone will we be if we have to wait the full time?"

I ran some calculations. "Forty-five minutes, give or take a couple of minutes."

"That long? But the drone just passed by a few minutes ago."

"Yeah, but its maximum thrust is a lot higher than ours *and* it has nowhere near our mass," I said. "On top of that, it made course corrections as soon as it exited the wormhole. We kept our initial heading when we went dark and it's almost at right angles with the correct course. By the time we get on course and reach the wormhole, we'll be way behind the drone."

"Do you think we still have a chance in Piscain?" Michelle asked.

"Yeah, I do," I answered. "We're going to come in with a different transponder, which might buy us a few minutes, and we only have to get to the closest wormhole before the navy catches us."

"How far is it to the closest wormhole and where does it go?"

I checked the charts. "It's a bit of a haul—seventeen light minutes—but that just means there won't be many ships around when we enter the system. And it goes to..." I checked the wormhole endpoint. "Um, it goes to Draconis."

"Where we *know* the Feds are looking for us." Michelle threw her head back and stared at the ship's ceiling. "Well, it will certainly be a lot easier sending those messages to our parents if we're in the same system."

"We could pick another wormhole. Maybe one clear across the system from where we come in?" I suggested.

"Won't that take us right through the heart of the hub and *way* too close to the naval base?"

"Yeah, but it has its advantages, too," I said.

"Really? Name one," Michelle countered.

"I'll give you two," I replied. "First, we've got plenty of fuel, so we can run at full thrust all the way in. By the time we pass the naval base, we'll be moving so fast no one will have a prayer of catching us unless they begin their own burn within our first thirty minutes in the system."

"And second?"

"No one will expect it, so any response will be concentrating on the closer wormholes." I cocked my head, considering a new twist to my idea. "We can start building velocity in this system and exit the wormhole going a lot faster than safety protocols demand."

Michelle stared off into space for a few seconds. "And what happens if a ship is in our way when we exit the wormhole? Or when we pass through the heavy traffic near the space station and the naval base?"

I shrugged. "Boom."

Something drew Michelle's attention back to the passive sensor display. "Hey, those two missiles just took off after the first one. We're safe to bring all ship's systems online and head for the wormhole to Piscain."

"How fast do you want me to go, hon?" I asked.

Michelle flashed her infectious grin. "Light her up and let's ride the fire, babe! We can always fire braking thrusters if we change our minds."

I brought the engines up to power and then gripped the throttle. "Should I turn off the inertial dampeners so we can really feel the acceleration?"

Michelle arched on eyebrow. "We're not going to be turned into red goo if you do that?"

"I wouldn't suggest it if it was dangerous. The acceleration will just be like a big hand pushing you back into your seat."

"So it will it be like when we ran away from Cummings' ship back in the Pegasus system?"

"Um..." Absently, I scratched my head and ran some basic math. "At a guess, the pressure will be about twice as strong as it was back then. This ship's engines have a lot more thrust than the *M&M* has."

"Last time I felt like I'd been punched in the gut—and you say this will be worse?" Michelle's other eyebrow rose to join the first one. "Do you think it's a good idea to do that sort of thing to the woman you love?"

"I'm going to say no."

Michelle smiled coquettishly. "Did your empathic ability tell you to say that?"

I shoved the throttle all the way forward and, unfelt by us, our ship surged toward the far away wormhole. "No, dear, that was just old fashioned common sense."

She laid her fingers lightly on my arm and lightly traced from my wrist to my shoulder. "Well, I'll make it worth your while if you can use your ability to make me feel something. Or use them to make me stop feeling something. I don't care which."

"I don't need my abilities to do *that*!" I laughed and tried pulling Michelle into my lap. To my surprise, she resisted.

The playful tone disappeared from her voice and she looked deeply into my eyes. "This time, you do."

Her tone brought me up short. The teasing and sexually playful tone were gone now, replaced by a very serious young woman. I took a deep breath, returned her gaze, and cleared my mind.

She pulled her hands away when I reached for them. "We know you can do that when we're touching. At least, sometimes. Try to do it without touching."

For the next fifteen minutes, I fought to rediscover the feeling I had in the bar back on Wolf. I think my ability touched Michelle a couple of times—just enough to make her take a quick breath, but not enough to make her really feel anything. When a bead of sweat trickled down my cheek, Michelle finally called a halt.

She kissed me gently. "It's a start, babe. We'll get there."

I hung my head, dejected and exhausted. "Maybe. But will we get there before Psi Corps catches up to us and hauls me away?"

"Psi Corps is most definitely *not* taking my husband from me!" The steel in Michelle's voice was reassuring. "And our children are most definitely *not* growing up without a father!"

I smiled at Michelle. "That's the first time either of us has mentioned children."

My wife bit her lip—a sure sign she was thinking about something. "You're right. Huh... You, um, do want children, don't you? I just sort of assumed-"

"Of course, I want children!" It was my turn to kiss her gently. "How could I not want to have a daughter with the most wonderful woman in the universe?"

"A daughter, huh?" Michelle cocked her head and smiled. "What if I want a son?"

"Just because our parents only had one child, doesn't mean we can't have more."

Michelle leaned over and rested her head on my shoulder. "Good answer."

Much later, the wormhole opened before us. Everything around us went gray as the ship plunged into the wormhole.

"It's three and a half hours to Piscain. Are there any other plans to concoct?" I asked.

Michelle shook her head. "But I can think of one thing we can do to pass the time."

"Good God, woman, is that all you think about when we're making a wormhole jump? Not that I'm complaining."

Michelle fended off my reaching hands. "That's not what I had in mind, Matt, though there's definitely a connection."

"I admit it, honey—you've lost me."

"Why don't we spend the next few hours figuring out names for those children we're going to have?"

I pretended to think for a few seconds. "I guess Michelle, Junior is right out?"

"Be serious, Matt. Please?"

Wrapping an arm around her, I said, "I'm sorry, honey. You have my undivided attention."

By the time we reached the end of our wormhole jump, we had four names selected, two for each sex. Then the ship's nav system gave the countdown and then we burst into the Piscain Hub.

# PISCAIN STATION

Hands poised over the ship's controls, I watched the sensor data roll in. Michelle and I both heaved sighs of relief when the sensors didn't show any ships lurking near the wormhole exit. We cut those sighs short as more sensor data arrived.

"Where did all those warships come from, Matt?" Michelle asked, her eyes glued to the sensor screen. "According to the system data, the base only has twenty-one naval ships stationed here. I've got close to a hundred on my screen."

"Damn, we *really* can't catch a break." I pounded the console before me for emphasis. "You can check the local news feeds to be sure, but it looks like the navy is running war games in the system."

"They've got squadrons spread all over the system, too," Michelle said, highlighting those on her screen. "I don't see how we can hope to get through to another wormhole."

"We've got to think of something." I studied the sensor display, hoping it would spark a useful idea. "It won't be very long before someone notices us and realizes we're going way too fast for safety."

Michelle bit her lower lip, a sure sign she was puzzling through the problem. "We need two plans—not one. The first is obvious—

we try for one of the other wormholes out of Piscain. Then we need a fallback plan if that doesn't work."

"I can't think of anything that doesn't involve me surrendering to Psi Corps to save your life, hon."

"Don't think I'm going to let you turn foolishly gallant on me, Matt." Michelle's voice held a hard edge. "I warned you about that kind of crap even before we left to rescue your parents."

"That's an odd sentiment coming from the girl who spent half her life ready to take a blaster bolt for me," I countered. "Look, I don't *want* to spend the rest of my life as a slave to Psi Corps, but I'll choose that over watching you die without a second thought."

Michelle glared at me for a few seconds and I glared right back at her. With an irritated shake of her head, Michelle broke eye contact.

"Fine. If you're determined to do that as a last resort, I guess I'd better figure out a next-to-last resort." She looked at the sensor screen again. "Will our current course take us close to Piscain Station?"

"Way too close," I replied. "Without a course change, we'll pass within a couple of kilometers of it."

"What if we abandon ship as we close on the station?" Michelle asked. "Can we use spacesuit thrusters or something to cross to the station and sneak onto it?"

I shook my head. "We would still carry all of the ship's velocity after exiting the ship. We'd fly right past the station and out into space where we'd either die or have to call for help—and I've already told you what I'll do if that happens."

"Is there any way we *can* make my idea work?" Michelle shrugged in frustration. "Fire braking thrusters before we jump or something?"

"Using reverse thrust would help, but..." I bent over my console and started calling up data. "If we reverse thrust while we're still a few hundred kilometers from the station, we can each take a jetpack and use those to slow down and maneuver to the station. It would be a long trip into the station, but we could do it."

"Okay, now we're talking!" Michelle exclaimed.

"Except that suits and jetpacks have their own transponders—for safety reasons," I added. "We'd need to disable those before powering up everything."

"Then hadn't you better get started on that, babe? Meanwhile, I'll figure out how to keep the navy off our backs for as long as possible." With a sudden smile, Michelle pulled out her data pad and tapped on the screen. After a few seconds, she grinned in triumph. "Ha! She's still here."

"Uh, *who* is still here, Michelle?" I asked, gathering the tools I needed.

"Mandy."

I drew a complete blank. "Who?"

"You don't remember Mandy?" Michelle's voice rose in pitch, taking on an over-excited, breathless tone. "I'm *so* hurt, George. How could you forget everything I did to get us out of the Pegasus system last year? I think Nancy Martin was right about you after all."

With those hints, it all came flooding back to me. Michelle playing the naive teenage girl to my lecherous man in his mid-twenties. The ingénue act earned 'Mandy' a fighter escort to a wormhole out of Pegasus system and 'George' a threatening lecture from then-Flight Commander Nancy Martin.

"Aren't those IDs blown now?" I asked. "Our rescue of my parents was really big news."

"You didn't follow any of those stories, did you, babe?" Michelle asked in return.

"No. I had a lot of other things on my mind—like spending time with my parents, settling into married life with you, and trying to figure out how to control my empathic abilities. Did I miss something?"

"Yep. Daddy made sure Nancy and her crew kept Mandy and George out of the story. Everyone else involved was a pirate, so those identities were preserved." Michelle actually giggled. "I kind of miss Mandy. She's such a sweet girl."

"Well, I don't miss George," I growled. "He was a jerk and a coward."

"Then you'll be happy to hear you don't have to play George again, babe."

"I don't? Who do I get to play?"

"Oh, you're still George," Michelle grinned, "but you don't have a speaking role."

"Okay..." I still couldn't figure out where Michelle was going with this. "Why don't I go work on those transponders and leave the acting to you?"

"That's probably a good idea, babe," she replied. "I'll put the comm unit on the ship's speaker system so you can hear what's going on."

I hefted my tools and headed aft.

"Oh, and George is unconscious, so try not to make any noise, babe," Michelle called after me.

"Why is George unconscious?" I asked.

"Because Mandy knocked him out, silly," Michelle replied. "The comm light just started blinking, Matt. Wish me luck."

Silently, I wished her luck. Then I offered up a prayer for us, wishing I could afford to broadcast the prayer into space just in case God couldn't hear prayers through a vacuum. The next few hours would decide if I remained free or faced a life of forced servitude.

As I started working on the transponder for my suit, Michelle switched on the ship's broadcast system and said, "Okay, Matt, I'm answering the comm. It's show time."

"Um, hello?" Michelle's normally confident voice was suddenly timorous. "Can you help me?"

"Identify yourself." The voice was male, brusque, and authoritative.

Michelle gave a startled squeak. "I'm, uh, Mandy. Are you—?"

"You are ordered to reduce velocity and prepare to be boarded."

Now we knew the message drone—or drones, more likely—sent by Captain Odenton was picked up. Worse, whoever was in charge in the Piscain Hub was taking the Captain's message very seriously.

"I can't do that!" Michelle said, her voice climbing higher with each syllable.

"Young woman, you not only *can* do it," the voice replied, "you *will* do it. If you do not comply, you will be fired upon."

"*What*? Y-you're going to sh-sh-shoot me?" From Michelle's voice, I could easily imagine tears streaming down Mandy's face. "B-b-but why?"

"Stop that blubbering at once, young woman. Do you hear me?" The voice all but barked the order. "No one will fire on your vessel if you simply do what you've been ordered to do."

"But I *can't*!" The tears gave way to a heart-wrenching wail. "I want to, but I *can't*!"

"What kind of nonsense is this?" the voice demanded. "Just pilot the ship."

"I don't know how." We were back to tears and little hiccupping breaths. "I'm not the pilot."

"Damnation, girl—just *tell* the pilot to do it." The voice exploded, what little patience the man had was obviously exhausted. "If he questions you, tell him those are orders from the Terran Federation Navy."

"I can't do *that*, either." Michelle went back to wailing, distress warring with confusion in her voice.

"For God's sake, girl, *why not*?" the man shouted.

"B-b-because he's unconscious. And tied up. And locked in a storage compartment." Michelle's voice gained strength with each word. By the end, she was shouting as well.

"Why the hell did you do that?" True confusion sounded in the man's voice and he was no longer yelling.

"Because he wanted to... And I said no and he got mad... Then he ripped my shirt and tore off my..." Michelle gulped and sniffed at each pause. Defiantly, she added, "So I hit him on the head with a big wrench. He didn't fall down so I hit him two more times. Then I dragged him to the storage room and taped his legs together and his hands behind his back."

"Christ almighty," the man murmured. "All right, young lady, please calm down. I'm sorry I yelled at you, but we thought your ship had criminals on board."

"This ship does have a criminal on board!" Michelle insisted in an offended tone. "Attempted rape is a crime, you know."

"Yes, I know miss... I'm sorry, what did you say your name was?"

"Mandy." Michelle let fear creep into her voice again. "Are you really going to shoot at the ship?"

"It's not my decision, but if you do your best to cooperate I'm sure everything will work out just fine." The man was less than convincing, to my ears. "Look, Mandy, we've got someone else who's going to talk to you, okay? A woman, because we think you'll be more comfortable talking about this to her."

And, right on cue, a woman said, "Okay, Jones, you're relieved. I've got the comm."

"Yes, ma'am," the man replied, sounding immensely relieved.

"Hi, Mandy," the woman said in a chipper tone. "Do you mind if I call you Mandy?"

"No... Um, what should I call you?" Wary uncertainty sounded in Michelle's response.

"My name is Jessica, but my friends call me Jess—and I hope we're going to be friends." When Jess continued, her voice was filled with concern. "Are you hurt?"

"Not really, no," Michelle replied in a small voice.

"Did the pilot—"

Disdain evident, Michelle said, "*George.*"

"George. Did he do more than *attempt* to force himself on you, Mandy?"

"No. I whacked him before he could do anything." Michelle's voice went small again. "Am I going to get in trouble for that?"

"Self-defense is not a crime," Jess replied, her voice maternal. "Honey, how old are you?"

"S-seventeen."

My head jerked up at that. Mandy was *sixteen*, I remembered that much. Then I went ahead and kicked myself. Ten months had passed since Mandy's last performance. Obviously, she'd had a birthday. Thank God Michelle remembered.

"Don't you think you're a little young to be out in a spaceship all alone with a boy?" Jess asked. "It *is* just the two of you, isn't it?"

"Uh huh. But George isn't a boy. He's twenty-five."

"I see." Jess's voice dropped about twenty degrees, leaving no doubt about her opinion of George. A commanding voice said something to Jess which I couldn't understand. "Mandy, I've got to ask you a quick question from my commanding officer. Did your sensors pick up any other spaceships when you were on the other side of the wormhole?"

"Yeah. There was something really fast and some missiles that hit a ship a long way away from us. We got really scared that it might be pirates, so George flew for the wormhole as fast as he could." Michelle's voice trembled again. "I was real happy to get into the wormhole until George... You know."

"Yes, Mandy, I know," Jess returned to her maternal tone of voice. "Tell you what, why don't we get your ship slowed down and then we can discuss what to do with George."

"But I already told that loud, rude guy that I don't know how to pilot the ship." Michelle let the tremor of building tears back into her voice.

"I know, honey." Jess continued in a cheerful tone, "But I've got a real pilot right here with me. The two of us are going to tell you exactly what to do. Okay?"

"O-okay. Um, he's not mean like that other guy, is he?"

A calm man's voice responded. "No, Mandy, I'm not mean. In

fact, I've got two daughters of my own. The oldest is only a couple of years younger than you."

"Oh." Michelle paused for a moment as if Mandy were thinking. "If, uh, your oldest daughter was where I am, would you be really mad at her?"

"No, Mandy, I'd be worried sick about her and I'd pray she was brave enough to do what you've done so far." The man paused for a second when his voice cracked. "And I'd hope she found people who could help her come home safely."

"People like Jess and you?"

"Exactly like Jess and me, Mandy."

My God, Michelle was good at this. Even knowing it was an act, I was drawn into the whole drama and found myself blinking away tears. I quickly got control of myself and put my full concentration into disabling the transponders in the suits and jetpacks.

"After you help me, you need to tell your daughters that you're a hero," Michelle said shyly. "Girls like having a hero daddy."

"Maybe I'll let you tell them, Mandy. Heroes aren't supposed to brag, you know," the pilot replied. His voice turned more business-like. "Now, let's get your spaceship slowed down. Okay?"

"Okay! Just tell me what to do."

"Are you sitting at the pilot's console, Mandy?" he asked.

"Yes, sir, I am," Michelle sounded just like a girl trying her best to be helpful.

"Good girl." The man's smile carried easily over the comm. "Do you see a panel labeled 'autopilot'?"

"Uh huh. It says the autopilot is engaged." Excitement crept into Michelle's voice as she relayed this information. "Does that mean it's turned on?"

"That's right, honey," the pilot said. "We're going to try the easiest fix first. It might not work, but that's okay. I want you to simply say 'Autopilot, fire braking thrusters.'"

Michelle repeated the words exactly. Our autopilot wasn't actually engaged, so nothing happened. Michelle relayed the news with disappointment.

"Don't worry, Mandy. A lot of autopilots are voice-keyed to keep people from accidentally giving orders to it." The man paused for a second as if thinking. "Is there a red button in the autopilot panel?"

"Yes, sir. Should I push it?"

"That will disengage—turn off—the autopilot," the man said. "Go ahead and push the button."

"Um, what does 'controls locked, enter pass code' mean?" Michelle asked, her voice rising again.

Three of the transponders were disabled, leaving just the one in the second jetpack. As I went to work on it, I marveled anew at Michelle's act. If the pass code idea held up, it might get us another ten minutes. I needed to get a look at our location to know for sure, but I thought we could safely abandon ship by now. If Michelle's latest deception did buy us ten minutes, our chances of making it to another wormhole were very good.

Jess responded to the question. "It means you have to get the pass code from George, Mandy."

"*No!*" Michelle shrieked. "If I open the door he might— I can't do that, Jess."

"Mandy, calm down, honey," Jess responded, her voice soothing. "You taped George up really tight, didn't you?"

Michelle sniffed. "Uh huh."

"Then George can't hurt you, Mandy." Jess kept her voice calm and controlled. "You can take the wrench, just in case you need to whack him again, but we really need that pass code."

"What if he won't wake up?" Michelle asked, returning to her small voice. "I hit him real hard."

"Take the portable med unit with you," Jess suggested. "Do you know how to use it?"

"Yeah, my Daddy showed me." Michelle sniffed again, as if ready to begin crying anew. "I miss my Daddy."

"I know you do, Mandy," Jess said. "But we need that pass code so we can get you back to him."

"O-okay, I'll try, Jess."

"You can do this, Mandy."

Michelle walked loudly away from the pilot console and came to see me. She punched open a closet door, keeping up her part, and called, "George? I've still got the wrench, so don't try anything. Hey, are you awake, George?"

Finished with her lines, Michelle whispered, "Are you done, babe?"

I nodded, closing up the final jetpack. I rose, handed Michelle's spacesuit to her, and whispered, "Go ahead and put this on. I want to be ready to go if we need to bail out."

Nodding, Michelle began pulling on the suit and called, "George?"

Pulling on my own suit, I almost missed the look she gave me. Interpreting it quickly, I moaned loudly. Michelle's answering smile told me I'd guessed right.

"Come on, George, wake up! I need the pass code."

Once again I rose to the occasion, moaning louder than before. On a whim, I added some nonsense syllables.

Michelle grinned and gave me a thumbs up. Then she motioned for me to do it all again. I gave an encore performance and then Michelle turned and headed back to the pilot chair.

In a quavering voice, Michelle said, "It's n-n-no good, Jess. I hit George too hard and he doesn't remember the pass code."

Jones was back on the comm, his voice business-like with undertones of anger. "You can cut the act, Mandy—if that's even your real name. We ran your voice print against the one Captain Odenton included in her message drone."

"Well, aren't you all sorts of clever," Michelle returned to her own voice. "Fine, you've figured out I was fooling you—but that's the only thing I've done wrong today. All my husband and I want to do is live our lives in peace. That's all we'd *been* doing until we made the mistake of fighting back when someone attacked us in a bar on Wolf. We are not criminals."

"Then you won't mind slowing down so we can get to the

bottom of this," the man replied. "If you're innocent, we'll have the two of you on your way as quickly as possible."

"And if we refuse?" Michelle asked.

"Then we will be forced to fire on you."

"You'd kill us for running from a bar fight?" Michelle put all of the incredulity she could muster into the question.

"No," the man replied evenly, "we'd kill you for knowingly concealing a rogue psychic."

Rogue psychic.

The Feds knew. Or at least they guessed. It shouldn't have surprised me after they chased us off Draconis, but actually hearing the accusation shook me in a way I hadn't expected. With effort, I listened to Michelle's response.

"Are you honestly talking about blowing our ship up because we *might* have a psychic..." Michelle paused for a second. When she continued, her voice was thick with sarcasm. "Excuse me, a *rogue* psychic—oooh, that's so much more sinister sounding—on board? That doesn't strike anyone as overkill?"

"Untrained, uncontrolled psychics are a danger to society, young woman," Jones replied, his voice harsh. "I cannot believe you are unaware of the Cairo Catastrophe. It's required teaching in all schools in the Federation."

"Yes, I'm aware of it. But just because *one* psychic went insane and panicked an entire city, doesn't mean anything," Michelle insisted. "That was four centuries ago, for God's sake."

"Which shows that Psi Corps works," Jones said.

"*Or* it shows that most psychics, like most regular people, aren't dangerous," Michelle countered.

As Michelle argued, I busied myself entering commands for the autopilot.

"I'm not going to discuss this with you any further," Jones declared. "You have one minute to comply with these orders or we will launch missiles."

"Go to hell!" Michelle snarled, slapping the off switch for the comm. She took a couple of seconds to regain control then turned to face me. "Is there any chance we can make it to a wormhole before the missiles get us?"

"If they launch missiles," Michelle gave me an exasperated look, so I quickly added, "which they probably will, but we can hope they don't. Anyway, no, we can't reach a wormhole before the missiles reach us. It's not even close."

Michelle bit her lip, something she only does when working through a problem, and nodded. "If Odenton included voice recordings in her messages, she almost certainly included logs of our escape, too. It's a safe bet the navy knows we can deal with a small number of missiles. If they attack, they'll use way more than three missiles... What will we need that we haven't already got stowed in the various suit compartments?"

"I've got tools and electronics to help me open any airlock we reach," I said, "and I stuffed all of our credit sticks into one of the pockets. What about the messages you wanted to send?"

"Already sent, though none of them include our plan to abandon ship," Michelle replied. "When we get into the space station, our first priority has *got* to be sending a follow-up message. If our parents hear a ship was destroyed in the Piscain Hub after the messages I've already sent..."

I hadn't even gotten that far in my thinking but tried for a knowing expression when I nodded. "Explaining all of this will be complicated. Can you create a coded message to cover it all?"

"Oh, yeah," Michelle waved my concern off without even thinking about it. "Daddy prepared a lot of different codes, including one that lets us encrypt any message."

Michelle and I turned to the sensor display as the last seconds of our one-minute warning ticked away. The time came and passed with nothing appearing on the display. Five seconds later, eight missile tracks blazed to life.

"Damn," I said. I activated the autopilot, then took Michelle's hand and led her to the airlock.

We helped each other attach the jetpacks to our suits then donned and sealed our helmets. I carefully inspected Michelle's suit, looking for poor seals and loose fastenings. Once I gave her the thumbs up, she did the same for me.

I led the way into the airlock and we waited as it cycled. When the outer hatch slid open, I leaned over and touched my helmet to Michelle's. "Are you ready?"

Keeping her eyes firmly fixed on mine, Michelle said, "Let's go."

Wrapping an arm around my wife, I used several clasps to hook our two suits together, and then jumped out into the void. We drifted away from the spaceship which, from our perspective, seemed as if it wasn't moving. Michelle closed her eyes and wrapped her arms tightly around me.

Making sure our helmets were touching again, I said, "I'm going to fire the jetpack for a bit, so we can get clear of our ship before the autopilot changes course. Keep holding on to me."

Michelle gave a short nod, so I fired the jetpack. It looked as if we pulled away from the spaceship, but I was decelerating while the ship maintained its velocity. In just a few seconds, it vanished from sight. I took a positional reading, adjusted our course a few degrees, and kept up my slow deceleration burn.

"Everything is looking good so far, hon," I said.

"Uh huh," Michelle said, her reply muffled.

Something, part empathic ability and part husband-senses, told me Michelle was having trouble with something. Fear spiked as I imagined all the myriad things which could go wrong.

"Michelle, what's wrong?" I asked. "Have you got a suit malfunction or something?"

"The suit is fine, babe," she said, her voice ragged.

Rather than ask anything more, I opened myself up and read Michelle. I expected to find a twinge of fear, but I found something else entirely. Michelle was absolutely terrified and her terror was building toward a full-on panic.

"Hon, what's wrong? I've never seen you anything more than mildly frightened before." I tried looking into her eyes, but they were squeezed tightly shut. "What's terrifying you?"

"Nothing," she whimpered. Michelle *never* whimpered. "Lots and lots of nothing. It just goes on and on and..." Michelle's voice broke and she began sobbing. "I thought I'd be okay, Matt. B-b-but all I can think of is floating away from you outside of Pegasus Station. Floating forever and ever and—"

Without conscious thought, my mind reached out to Michelle. It grabbed her terror and gently eased it out of her mind entirely. I steeled myself for my own bout of fear as I pulled her emotion into my own mind—and the terror hit hard for a second after I pulled it in. Then it changed. Michelle's blob of emotion—for want of a better phrase—just felt uncomfortable. It sort of sat in the corner of my mind and pulsed.

"*Oh!*" Michelle breathed a soon as the fear left her. "Matt, that was you, wasn't it?"

"Of course. Do you see any other rogue psychics nearby?"

"That was..." Michelle's arms squeezed me even more tightly. "Thank you, babe. I don't..."

"I couldn't let you suffer like that, Michelle. Not when I could stop it."

Michelle looked at me, her eyes shining. "But how did you—?"

I shook my head. "I don't really know. I just wanted to ease your fear and next thing I knew it was inside my head."

"But why aren't you terrified?" Michelle asked. "When you absorbed all that anger, it had a real effect on you."

"My best guess is that I'm not scared of space. Not even your abject terror of it can overcome it." Another idea occurred to me. "Or maybe my power has a way to wall off stolen emotions, provided I don't absorb a whole bar-full of the emotion. Either way, I think I can keep you fear-free until we reach the base."

"Have I told you just how much I love you, Matt?"

"Every single time you look at me, hon." I grinned at my wife. "It's too bad we're stuck in these spacesuits. This would be a really great time to get naked together."

"Yeah, sex in zero gravity sounds interesting," Michelle said, laughing. "Sex in zero atmosphere, not so much."

The rest of the trip to Piscain Station was anticlimactic. Michelle's ball of terror stayed out of my way and my course to the station was accurate. We took our time maneuvering around the huge station, hunting for an underused, out-of-the-way airlock. Finally, Michelle spotted one.

"I don't know how you managed to see that door, hon," I marveled at her eyesight, "but it looks perfect."

"I don't know, either," she said. "It just jumped into focus."

To my surprise, the outer hatch wasn't locked. "Let's get inside and get out of these suits."

We cycled through the airlock and into a suit prep room. We removed our helmets and gave each other a big kiss.

"That's real sweet," a young, male voice said, "but you're running late and a maintenance crew is due here in six minutes. We've got to be gone before they get here."

Looking toward the voice, I saw a teenage boy about fifteen years old. He was slender and already as tall as I am. Bright brown eyes looked at us from under a head of brown hair and his clothes were typical for someone his age. The boy slouched in the corner of the room, attempting a casual air belied by the tension evident in his face.

"Who are you?" I asked.

"I'm the guy who unlocked the airlock and made sure Michelle noticed the hatch when you got close enough to see it," he replied. The boy shoved off the wall and pointed to a row of lockers against the other wall. "You can put your spacesuits in lockers fourteen and fifteen. No one will disturb them before we can come back for them."

"How do you know my name?" Michelle asked as the two of us began pulling off our suits.

"You and Matt are all Cassandra has been able to talk about for the last month. She insisted I case this airlock six times to make sure everything was in place for you."

The boy opened locker fourteen and started stowing Michelle's gear inside. With a half-shrug, Michelle accepted his help. The kid stacked the last of Michelle's gear and immediately began helping me with mine.

Handing my helmet to him, I said, "Even in light of everything that's happened to us lately, that makes no sense at all."

"Yeah, welcome to my world," the boy muttered.

"Okay..." I said, unsure what he meant by that.

The kid checked his chrono every fifteen seconds, telegraphing a need for haste. Or maybe he just wanted to give us that impression. Either way, it worked. Shutting locker fifteen, I said, "Let's go."

The kid led us out of the prep room without bothering to make sure the coast was clear. Exchanging puzzled looks, Michelle and I followed him. The guy set a fast pace like he really did want to get away from the airlock before a maintenance team showed up.

"What are you reading off of him?" Michelle whispered. At normal volume, she asked, "You know our names. Shouldn't you tell us yours?"

"Oh yeah, sorry—Zav told me to do that. I'm Gene."

"I'd return the favor, but it seems like you already know all about us," I said. "Thanks for unlocking the airlock, though."

We turned a corner and lost sight of the door to the airlock's prep room. Seconds later, voices sounded from down that corridor as a group of men and women entered the hallway we'd just left. Their discussion was technical and left little doubt they were a maintenance team.

"The rest of the way should be clear until we reach the public part of the station." Gene slowed to a normal walking pace. He looked over his shoulder at me. "You can stop trying to read me, Matt. Empaths and telepaths don't mix well."

My mind whirled, trying to figure out what question I wanted to ask first. Michelle beat me to it, asking, "You know Matt is an empath? And you're admitting to us you're a telepath?"

Gene nodded. "Zav said I should mention that at the same

time I mentioned Matt's ability. He said it would make you less anxious if you knew I was a rogue psychic, too."

"Thank you. That's pretty brave of you, telling that kind of thing to strangers," Michelle said. "If you can't read empaths, how did you know Matt was trying to read you?"

"It was an easy guess. I mean, I've been trying to read him," Gene replied.

Michelle gave Gene an appraising look. "That's reasonable, Gene, but it's not the full truth, is it?"

The kid blushed. "Um, no."

Michelle took my hand. "Did you read anything besides my surface thoughts?"

"No—I'd never do anything that rude!" A shocked expression came over Gene. "At least not to friends. I don't blame you for holding hands with Matt, though."

Michelle's eyebrows rose. "So you know that lets Matt's ability shield most of my thoughts from you? And why are you calling us friends? I mean, you seem like a nice enough guy, but we just met you."

"*You* just met *me*. I feel like I've known you for a year and a half —ever since Cassandra first told us about the two of you." The corners of Gene's mouth curled up into a smile. "She was really upset Zav wouldn't take her to either of your weddings."

"Okay, I'm completely confused, Gene," I said. "Michelle and I weren't even a couple a year and a half ago. How could this Cassandra—"

Stopping at a door, Gene interrupted me. "Through this door is one of the shopping districts. I know you've got a lot of questions, but the answers are going to have to wait until Zav can explain everything."

Then Gene punched the door control. With a hiss, the door slid aside and a wall of sound rolled into the hallway. With a jerk of his head, Gene strolled out into the crowded shopping district. Seeing no other good options, we followed him.

The sights, sounds, and crowd in the shopping district

shouldn't have been jarring to me—I grew up on the second most populous planet in the Federation, after all—but Michelle and I spent most of the last three weeks together on the spaceship. Ex-spaceship, I realized, as the navy's missiles had surely blasted the ship to atoms by now. But, other than an all-too-brief stop on sparsely settled Wolf, neither of us had been around other people in a while. I found myself jumping at unexpected sounds and unable to concentrate on much besides following Gene.

Michelle leaned in close and spoke in a low voice. "How are you doing, babe? Is my little ball of terror causing problems? If you need to release it, I'm pretty sure I can handle it now."

I'd had the clump of emotion off in the corner of my mind long enough I no longer even thought about it. Prompted by Michelle's words, I checked on it. "Um, it's gone, hon."

"Gone? Where did it go?" she asked.

"Damned if I know, Michelle," I answered. "Maybe it just slowly leaked away while I wasn't concentrating on it? Or maybe it vanished when we entered the airlock and your reason to be terrified disappeared. I don't know a lot about this stuff."

Gene drifted back to walk next to us during that exchange. At my last statement, he grinned. "Don't worry, Zav knows all about it." Pointing to a corridor on the right, he added, "We go that way."

"You know, I'm getting tired of all of these veiled hints about people we've never met who seem to know a lot about us," I said, my temper rising. "Why should we trust you?"

"Because I really do want to help," Gene insisted.

Most public access space station corridors have regular alcoves so pedestrians can stop and chat without blocking foot traffic. I stepped into one, pulling Michelle along with me. Gene followed, refusing to wilt under my glare.

Before I could speak, Gene asked in a low voice, "Will it help if I let you read me?"

In surprise, I responded with a question of my own. "You can do that?"

"It's not easy and I'm not real good at it," Gene answered, "but I think I can let you in for a few seconds. Zav's been working with me on it."

"Let me guess," Michelle said. "It's because Cassandra told him we might not trust you?"

"It didn't take a precog to figure out you might get suspicious," Gene said. The boy closed his eyes and slowly his entire body relaxed. "Okay, try it now."

I took Gene's hand, pretending to examine it for some kind of injury. I struggled to calm my own mind. Michelle, obviously sensing my difficulties, gently rubbed my back. The simple normalcy of that helped. I established a tentative contact with Gene, but immediately ran into interference from his telepathy.

"I can't get through, Gene," I said

"I'm trying," he hissed.

Without hesitation, Michelle used her free hand to start kneading one of Gene's shoulders. The contact surprised him and his eyes flew open.

"I trust you will be a gentleman, Gene," Michelle whispered, smiling her brightest smile, "and respect my privacy."

Gene melted under her smile and the gentle massaging of his shoulder. As he smiled in response, his interference dropped away. It only lasted a few seconds, but it was enough. Michelle raised an eyebrow in question as I released Gene's hand. I smiled and nodded.

"Thank you, Gene," Michelle said. "Lead on."

It took us another twenty minutes and half a dozen different turns before Gene stopped at a door. With a big grin, he keyed the door open.

"Matt, Michelle—welcome home."

# CASSIE

As the door slid aside, Gene motioned for us to enter. Unable to ignore her bodyguard training, Michelle stepped in front of me and entered first. She immediately came backpedaling out, forcing me to brace myself and catch her.

"You're here! You're here! You're here!" The voice held the excited high pitch of a prepubescent girl and came from somewhere around Michelle's chest. Two small arms wrapped tightly around my wife's waist. "I've been waiting *so* long to meet you in person and now you're here!"

Michelle glanced over her shoulder at me, grinned, and wrapped her arms around the source of the voice. "I'm happy to meet you, too, Cassandra."

"Call me Cassie." The excited face of a girl about twelve years old peeked around Michelle's side. Deep brown eyes shone at me from under brunette bangs. "Hi, Matt. I'm glad you're here, too."

"Pleased to meet you, Cassie," I said. "I only wish everyone was as happy to see us as you are."

"Here's an idea, Cassie," Gene said. "Why don't you stop blocking the door and let us in?"

"Oops. Sorry. I'm just so excited." Giggling, the girl unwrapped her arms from Michelle, took Michelle's hand, and pulled her inside. "Come on—I want to show you my room."

Michelle laughed, allowing the energetic girl to tow her through the living room and down the hall. "I'll, uh, be in Cassie's room if you need me, Matt."

Closing the corridor door behind us, Gene said, "Wow, Cassie is even more excited than I thought. Sorry about that."

I waved it off. "No worries. Is this Zav you talked about around?"

"I don't know. Hang on." Raising his voice, Gene called, "Cassie —where's Zav?"

The girl's voice came back, "He went shopping and took Kristin and Mark with him."

"I thought he wanted to meet Matt and Michelle as soon as possible," Gene replied.

"Yeah, but he claimed I was so excited I was driving him crazy and he had to get out before I succeeded," Cassie said. "Kristin and Mark begged him to take them, too."

Gene glanced at me, pulling out his comm. "I'll call Zav and tell him you're here."

"Matt?" Michelle called from Cassie's room. Her voice sounded strained, so I was on my way down the hall before she even said, "Can you come here?"

Cassie's room looked like an average preteen girl's room, except almost every inch of wall space was filled with sketches. I gave the art a quick glance, impressed at the talent displayed by the artist. Looking at the girl, I asked, "Did you draw all of these? They're very good."

Nodding, Cassie beamed with pleasure at my compliment.

"Babe, have you actually *looked* at the drawings?" Michelle asked, her voice still thin and brittle.

I went to Michelle, looked where she was looking, and felt my blood run cold. Two drawings, slightly set apart from the others, showed a young man lying in a pool of blood and a young woman weeping over a grave. The young man was me. The young woman was Michelle. The grave was mine.

Her voice still bright, Cassie said, "Don't worry about that, Michelle. It only happened if Matt never told you he was an empath. I didn't really know you, then, so I didn't put much work into it."

My eyes drifted over the rest of the art. All of it was about Michelle and me and an unsettling number of them ended with one or both of us dead. The next series was on Rockport Station and showed both of us dead in the hanger where Paco and his gang ambushed us.

"That's what happened if you only shot Paco one time," Cassie told me. "I was getting to know you by then, so I'm really glad you shot him three times."

She pointed to the next set of drawings, which showed the *M&M* making a run around Hector's mining ships in an attempt to reach the wormhole. It ended with our ship exploding under the combined fire of all of the mining sleds.

"I was *so* happy when Michelle thought of running for that debris field," Cassie continued, oblivious to the effect her artwork had on Michelle and me.

Cassie had another dozen sets of drawings, all of them similar to what we'd already viewed. The worst of the lot was a haunting sketch of Michelle, obviously dead and with ice crystallizing on her skin, drifting in space. Some of the drawings were happy—me and my parents hugging, Michelle and me walking down the aisle after our fancy wedding on Draconis—but a lot of them were unsettling in the extreme. One of the last sets showed two Federation agents taking me away while two more agents restrained a distraught Michelle.

I turned an appalled gaze on Michelle, but she was looking past me to a section of wall I hadn't gotten to yet. Her eyes twitched rapidly back and forth. Turning, I realized what held her attention. One drawing was set in the room we'd walked through to reach Cassie's room. The crumpled, bloody bodies of Cassie, Gene, an older man, a teenage boy, a teenage girl, Michelle, and me lay scattered around the room. The other drawing showed a room I'd never seen. An older Cassie, maybe in her late teens, played with two very young girls as Michelle and I walked out a door.

"Don't worry, I'm free that night," Cassie said.

"What?" Michelle forced her eyes away from the drawings and looked at Cassie.

"To babysit Nancy and Nora," Cassie continued. "I'll always be free to babysit your children."

Michelle's wide eyes met mine over the girl's head. In a whisper, she said, "But we just *chose* those names a day or two ago."

"I know you did, or I wouldn't have told you," Cassie added. "I wouldn't want you to think *I* named your babies."

"We're going to have babies? Two girls?" I asked.

"Unless we all end up dead in the living room, yeah," Cassie replied. She tilted her head and scratched her chin. "If we don't die, you might have more babies. I haven't seen anything besides those two possibilities. Not yet, anyway." Then Cassie pulled both of us into a hug. "Whatever happens, at least I got to meet you two first."

The voice of a middle-aged man came from the doorway. "I meant to be here when you arrived. Meeting Cassie without a little advance preparation can be...unsettling."

Cassie blew a raspberry at the man. "I just showed them all the stuff that *could* have happened. It *didn't* happen, so why should it bother them?"

"Spoken like a true precognitive, Cassie." Looking at the speaker, I wasn't surprised to see the older man from Cassie's drawing of the corpse-filled living room. Entering the room, he held out his hand. "I'm Zavier Gordon, but everyone just calls me Zav."

Taking his hand, I said, "I get the feeling it would be a waste of breath giving you our names."

Michelle interrupted. "I don't want to sound rude, but let's skip the formalities and get busy packing." Jerking her thumb at the macabre drawing of the living room, she added, "That particular future can't happen if we leave, right?"

"Precognition is more complicated than that, I'm afraid. Leaving may simply cause the event to change scenes, as well," Zav said. "But I'm afraid that's a moot point. We can't leave."

"Why not?" Michelle demanded.

Zav's face turned grim. "The Federation Navy has shut down all departures from the system while they investigate the destruction of your ship."

"Okay. That gives us more time to prepare for our departure," Michelle said.

"I wouldn't count on that. The navy has access to some very sophisticated sensors," Zav responded. "The chances are very good that they'll discover no one was on board when the ship blew up."

"And *that* means the Feds will search Piscain Station for Matt and me." Michelle dropped onto Cassie's bed, her head held in her hands. "The five of you are in danger and it's all our fault."

Cassie dropped onto the bed next to Michelle and hugged her. "Don't cry, Michelle. You didn't put us in danger."

Michelle forced a smile as the first tear spilled out of her eye and ran down her cheek. "That's sweet of you, Cassie, but we both know that's not true."

"Neither of you knows any such thing, Michelle," Zav said. "Danger waxes and wanes around us with the frequency of Terra's moon. Your arrival simply signals a period of waxing danger for us."

"Zav's right, Michelle," Cassie added. "We'll tell you our story over dinner and you'll see. Oh, and it's my turn to help cook." Giving Michelle a last squeeze, Cassie hopped up. "Besides, don't you need to send a message home?"

"Oh my gosh, you're right. I—" Michelle broke off and gave Cassie a wondering look. "Did you 'see' me sending a message home, just like you saw us coming in through that airlock?"

"Nah. It's just what I'd do if I had parents who love me and were worried about me." A wistful look stole over Cassie's face, disappearing almost as quickly as it came. The girl flashed a grin and tapped her head. "Besides, I'm just that smart."

Wiping her eyes, Michelle laughed as the girl dashed out of the door. Looking at Zav, she said, "Cassie is quite something. The only people who have ever made me feel as welcome as she did are my family."

"To Cassie, you *are* family. She's been having visions of you two for the last year and a half—almost to the exclusion of anything else." Zav's gaze followed the girl down the short hallway. "Before that, her visions were all over the place—some of them concerned us, but most of them had no apparent connection to anything or anyone familiar. I thought it would be the same as usual when she first told me about the 'nice rich boy looking for his parents' with 'the most beautiful girl in the galaxy' at his side."

Michelle actually blushed at Zav's words. "That's very sweet of Cassie, but even I know I'm not *that* beautiful."

"Well, *I* think Cassie shows amazing perception for one so young," I said.

"You are a very pretty woman, Michelle," Zav said, "but what Matt said is true. Cassie's gift lets her see people differently than the rest of humanity sees people. It's not just a person's outward appearance she sees. There are times when a single vision can tell Cassie who a person was and, more importantly, who they will be. Until you two entered her visions, she rarely saw the same person twice. Now, it's entirely possible she knows you better than you know yourself."

Zav stepped to Michelle's side, put one hand on each of her shoulders, and looked in her eyes. "Cassie loves me like a favorite uncle, and I treasure that. She loves you and Matt even more—like you're her brother and sister or maybe even her parents."

Zav's announcement stunned Michelle and me. For once, I found my tongue first. "What about Cassie's real parents? Even if she hasn't seen them in a long time, surely she loves them more than us. I was apart from my parents for seven years, but my love for them never dimmed."

Zav grimaced. "Cassie's power manifested at a very early age—much too early for her to understand what was happening. She started talking about strange people and stranger happenings when she was four. Her parents never quite figured out what their daughter was talking about though they found her rambling disturbing. When Cassie was five, they found her crying over the death of another child in their neighborhood—only the child was playing outside right then. The next morning her parents learned the child was killed in a flyer accident a few hours after they found Cassie crying. They immediately took their 'creepy daughter' to the nearest Psi Corps office, turned her in, claimed the reward, and just walked away."

"What kind of parents could do that to their own child?" Michelle wondered, her voice barely more than a horrified whisper. "Did she tell you about it?"

"No. I was there," Zav replied. As Michelle and I exchanged alarmed looks, Zav held his hands up in a placating gesture. "I was going to build up to that, but once again Cassie has precipitated a change in plans. I used to work for Psi Corps—and that's why I have more reason to hate them than even you do."

A girl about the same age as Gene poked her head into the room. She was petite, with raven hair, gray eyes, and an impish smile. "You can trust Zav. Really."

"Thank you, Kristin," Zav said. Turning to us, he added, "Kristin is a telekinetic. She's developing quite a deft touch, too."

"Did I hear Cassie say Michelle needs to send a message?" Kristin asked. "She can borrow my makeup to disguise herself, and I'll be happy to take her to a message center."

"Thank you, Kristin," Michelle said, heading for the door. Over her shoulder, she said, "And Matt, I don't need to tell you to stay inside and out of sight, do I?"

"Don't worry, Michelle," Zav said before I could play the part of the put-upon husband, "I'll keep Matt busy until you get back."

"Doing what?" I asked.

"We'll start with you telling me everything you've learned and done with your empathic ability," he replied, "then we'll get started on your training."

That brought Michelle up short. Spinning, she asked, "What makes you qualified to train my husband?"

Zav gave a bitter smile. "I was one of Psi Corps' psychic trainers before I ran off with their four most promising young psychics."

I felt a surge of excitement. "And you know how to train empaths, too?"

"You'll be my tenth, Matt."

"Can you teach him how to defeat the test for psychic abilities?" Michelle asked, her eyes full of hope.

Zav shook his head, "I'm afraid that's impossible. But don't worry, there is a lot I *can* teach him."

Disappointed, Michelle turned and followed Kristin into the hallway. Zav and I went down to the living room where, amidst the sounds of kids cooking and two girls discussing makeup, Zav began my training.

Zav questioned me in detail about my empathic abilities, how I discovered them, and my early experiences with them. I was describing how we'd used Michelle's idea of pointing toward my parents when Kristin and another girl came into the living room. The double take I performed when I realized the other girl was Michelle must have been comical since both girls laughed. Looking through the changes in makeup and the done-up hair, I readily recognized my wife. If I'd just glanced at her as she walked past me, I'd never have known it was her.

"You did a good job with the makeup, Kristin," Michelle said. "Even Matt was fooled for a second."

"The makeup and the hair are certainly part of it, hon, but I'm still trying to figure out what else is different," I said. "I mean, you're *you*, but you're also *not* you—if that makes any sense."

Michelle ticked off on her fingers, "Putting my hair up changes my neckline. The makeup changes my face. The clothes aren't my typical fashion. I'm wearing high heels, which changes my height, and they're too small for my feet, which changes the way I walk."

Zav nodded his approval. "Those shoes also give you an awkward gait which will put people in mind of a younger girl who is just getting used to walking in heels. If station security has video footage of you, these changes ought to be enough to throw off their recognition programs. But Kristin, where did you get such a short skirt for her to wear? I've told you—"

"The skirt was several centimeters longer than this, Zav. I made a few modifications," Michelle said.

"Why would you do such a thing?" Zav asked.

Instead of answering, Michelle bent over and gave me a quick kiss on the lips. As she did that, I heard a couple of strangled sounds coming from the kitchen. Glancing around Michelle, I saw Gene and a boy a couple of years younger than him—Mark, no doubt—staring goggle-eyed at Michelle's backside.

"Michelle, it might not be a good idea for you to bend so far over while wearing that skirt," I said, trying to sound as casual as possible.

Michelle straightened, pulled down the hem of the skirt, and smiled at the boys. The two were blushing furiously and looking everywhere except at Michelle. She said brightly, "Oh good, it works."

"Um, what works, hon?"

"Sometimes a distraction is just the thing a girl needs." Michelle patted my cheek. "Fortunately, guys are visually oriented and *so* predictable. Give them a look up a girl's skirt and their eyes can't help but go there. That kind of thing might only gain me a couple of seconds, but that's forever in certain situations."

"Just so we're clear," I asked, "you're planning to flash half of Piscain Station as a distraction?"

"Only if it's necessary to keep you and these kids safe," Michelle said, spinning about and tottering to the door. Just before she opened the door, she gave me a dead serious look. "Babe, I would happily stroll naked down the busiest street on Draconis if it would help keep you safe."

The door slid open and the two girls left the apartment. Watching the door slide shut, I whispered, "That's fair, hon. I'd happily die to keep you safe."

From the kitchen, Cassie sighed, "See? I *told* you they were really romantic."

Zav stared at the door for a few seconds then gave himself a shake. He gave me a sheepish grin and a shrug. Like the boys in the kitchen, Michelle's stunt with the skirt also drew Zav's eyes. I shrugged in return, accepting his unspoken apology for ogling my wife.

"Now, Matt, you were telling me about how you used your ability to find your parents. I must say that was an inspired suggestion on Michelle's part. I've never heard of an empath doing such a thing before."

"Maybe that's because all of the other empaths you've met were in Psi Corps' hands and no longer had anyone they wanted to find?" I suggested.

Without waiting for an answer, I continued with my story. Zav asked probing and insightful questions, particularly when I described how I broke through my unconsciously self-imposed wall. I had to do that so my ability could lead me to Michelle as she drifted in space outside of Pegasus Station. But when I told him about the bar on Wolf, his attention sharpened. I finally wrapped up by telling him how I absorbed Michelle's panic outside of Piscain Station.

"You've left something out, Matt," Zav said. "I'm not sure what it is, but you stumbled a bit between your parental pointing, as you call it, in the Pegasus system and the ones on the station. I need to know everything about your ability if I'm going to train you."

I nodded, feeling color rising in my cheeks. "What I left out is the first time Michelle and I...um, you know."

Zav smiled. "Alone on a spaceship with the girl of your dreams? I'm surprised it took you that long."

"Yeah, anyway... I was able to read Michelle while we were doing it, of course. But Michelle also read *me* at the same time. Or I projected my feelings into her." It was my turn to grin sheepishly and shrug. "I wasn't really paying attention to my empathic ability at the time."

His eyes far away, Zav said, "No doubt, Matt. No doubt."

"Anyway, that's all I can think of to tell you. Does it help?"

Zav's eyes focused on me. "Absolutely. You're a rare find, Matt. A rare find, indeed!"

"How so?" I asked.

"The first projecting empath on record is the unfortunate man behind the Cairo Catastrophe, several centuries ago." Seeing my eyes widen in reaction to this news, Zav quickly added, "You're not like that man at all, Matt. He was completely insane, for one thing, and far more powerful than you, for another. Not that you aren't powerful, mind you, but he projected his insanity into millions of people."

"That's good because I don't ever want that kind of power."

"Projecting empaths are rare. Most of them can't do much more than sway emotions a little bit. What you did with Michelle is quite impressive. But you are the *only* empath I've heard of who could draw the emotions of others into himself." Zav stroked his chin, deep in thought. "It's obvious I can skip a lot of basic training with you, but I've also got to figure out how to exercise your projection and absorption abilities—assuming the Feds give us time to train you."

Cassie, who had been spending more time listening to my story than helping in the kitchen, said, "I told you they were fascinating people, Zav."

He smiled at the girl. "That you did, my dear."

"If you've got what you need right now," I said to Zav, "I'm going to help Cassie in the kitchen."

Zav waved me toward the others, his eyes already drifting out of focus.

I wasn't particularly useful in the kitchen—Cassie had to show me how to do just about everything—but she chattered happily with me about anything and everything. She also made me tell her how I proposed to Michelle, proclaiming it the most romantic story she'd ever heard. Then I told her about using my ability to find Michelle after she was thrown off into space and that became the most romantic story in the universe. Talking to Cassie and the boys made the time pass quickly. And before I knew it, Kristin and Michelle were back.

"Did you have to flash anyone while sending the message, hon?" I asked, turning to greet her.

"No, I didn't have any trouble sending the message, Matt. But we've got real problems." Her face troubled, Michelle kicked off the too-small shoes and laid her head on my shoulder. "Video images of us are up all over the station. Worse, the Feds are already mobilizing to search the station for us."

The four young psychics began talking at once. Cassie, Gene, and Mark threw rapid fire questions at Kristin. In between randomly answering some of their questions, Kristin launched into a breathless description of her trip with Michelle. My mind spun, searching for a way we could escape from the Federation net closing around the station. Michelle bit her lip, showing she was also searching for some solution to our problem.

"That's *enough*! All of you be silent." Zav's raised voice cut through the babble, which immediately ceased. "Thank you. Cassie, Gene, please serve dinner."

"But Zav," Cassie implored, "this is—"

A sharp glance from Zav cut her off in mid-sentence. "What is the rule of the household, Cassandra?"

Upon hearing Zav use her full first name, Cassie's impatience faded to resignation. "We don't discuss problems at the dinner table."

"Right—and there are no exceptions to that rule." Zav's eyes met the gazes of each of his charges. "Is that clear?"

"Yes, Zav," all four intoned.

"What a lovely idea," Michelle said brightly. Pulling away from me, she added, "I'm going to change out of this too-short skirt, so save me a seat next to you, babe."

Gene and Mark looked decidedly disappointed at Michelle's announcement while Zav appeared relieved. All three pairs of eyes watched as she walked down the hall to Kristin's room. Okay, *my* eyes tracked her gently swaying backside and long legs, too.

At the door, Michelle gave a quick glance at us, smiled knowingly, and said, "Do you see what I mean about men, Kristin?"

Kristin's wide eyes swept back and forth among the four males in the room. "Yep. You're right."

"What is she right about?" Cassie asked.

In a stage whisper, Kristin said, "I'll tell you when you're a little older."

"I think we'll discuss this now, young lady," Zav said.

Michelle's voice drifted down the hall, "We don't discuss problems at the dinner table, Zav. No exceptions."

Zav's eyebrows climbed so high they vanished under his hairline, causing all four of the young psychics to burst out laughing. A rueful smile spread across his lips. "Ah, the ignominy of having my own words turned against me in my own home. All right, you rapscallions, let's eat."

Cassie pointed to a chair for me, left an empty seat next to it for Michelle, and then sat down on the other side of the empty chair. The others took their own seats, with Michelle joining us just as Zav sat at the head of the table. Zav rapped his knuckles twice on the table and all talk ceased. Mark said a quick blessing, ending with the request, "And please keep our family and our guests safe."

The others all said, "Amen."

Released from the pre-meal ritual, the four kids directed a barrage of questions at Michelle and me, all the while spooning food onto plates and passing serving dishes around the table.

"Children, let our guests eat," Zav said, his voice rising over the hubbub.

"But we want to learn how they got here," Mark said, a little teenage whine entering his voice.

"That's fair," I replied, "but only if you guys tell us your story after we tell ours."

Michelle and I took turns telling the story of our flight from Draconis and then Wolf, finishing with the long space-suited flight to Piscain Station. The four kids were suitably impressed when Michelle told them how I drew the fear right out of her. When we got to the point where we met Gene, we wrapped it up.

"Your turn," Michelle said to the others.

Their tale proved as harrowing as you might expect, with hair's breadth escapes and many different homes, and began when Cassie's parents brought her to the Psi Corps offices. Already disillusioned with his employer, Zav patiently formulated an escape, taking the best psychics in his facility at the time.

"I hated leaving any children behind," Zav said, pain etched on his face.

"He did it 'cause I warned him," Cassie said around a mouthful of food. "I had dreams about him and we all got killed if he tried to take anyone else."

"That she did," Zav continued. "You can imagine how surprised I was when this five-year-old girl told me she knew what I was planning *and* what would happen if I overreached—though she didn't use that word. Utilizing their unique talents, we were able to procure passage on a spaceliner and, for the most part, stayed off the Federation's scanners ever since."

"We know about Cassie's, Kristin's, and Gene's abilities," Michelle said. "What about you, Mark?"

In response, Mark just grinned widely at Michelle. To my considerable surprise, my wife's voice filled with chagrin. "Oh, that was so rude of me to suspect anything from such a fine young man. Can you ever forgive me, Mark?"

I looked at Michelle and grabbed her hand. "Are you okay, hon?"

Michelle's eyes widened just as Gene smacked Mark on the back of the head. "We don't use our powers on friends, dumbass."

"Ow!" Mark said, rubbing his head. But he also lowered his eyes and muttered, "I'm sorry. I just thought it would be easier if I showed her."

"What did you do to her?" I demanded.

"I'm a charismatic. I can make people like me and sort of get them to do what I want," Mark said. "I can't make anyone do anything that they're really opposed to—like make a good person kill someone, for instance. But I bet I could get Michelle to bend over again while she was wearing that short skirt." This time it was Kristin who smacked Mark on the back of the head. "How did you stop my ability from working on Michelle?"

I shrugged. "I just took her hand. Empaths tend to screw up telepathic powers. I assume your ability is just a specialized form of telepathy?"

"It is," Zav said. "And Mark, you get kitchen duty for a week for using your abilities on Michelle."

The boy nodded his head and his shoulders drooped. "I really am sorry."

"I believe you and I forgive you," Michelle said. "But aren't you also the solution to all our problems? Can't we just have Mark use his abilities on whoever comes to search the apartment and make them go away?"

"I wish it were that simple," Zav said. "His ability is extremely useful, but it won't deter someone who is following specific orders. The searchers will feel badly when they insist on performing the search, but they'll still do it. No, we need some other way to get around this."

"What if Matt and I hide in service tunnels or get in with the vagrant population?" Michelle asked.

"What vagrant population?" Gene asked.

"Pegasus Station had a pretty large one," Michelle replied. "I just assumed..."

"Piscain Station authorities don't allow that kind of thing,"

Gene said. "That's one reason why there are so many sensors all around the station—including in the service tunnels."

Michelle blew out an exasperated breath and gave me a lopsided grin. "Well, babe, can you maybe suck out the searchers' curiosity or something equally crazy?"

I surprised Michelle by giving her suggestion serious consideration. "You might actually have something, hon. If we hide in one of the bedrooms—under a bed or in a closet—I might only have one searcher to deal with. If he's not curious while he's searching the room, maybe he'll just give it a quick look and move on."

I looked at Zav. "What do you think? Can you help me enhance that ability to the exclusion of anything else?"

Zav gave the idea careful thought before finally nodding. "I think it's worth trying though projecting impatience in conjunction might improve the odds."

Cassie leaned across Michelle and hugged me. "I *knew* one of you would save the day."

"They haven't saved the day yet, Cassie," Zav said. "And while I get started with his training, you need to do the dishes."

"If you don't mind," Michelle said, "I'll help."

Cassie brightened at the prospect of doing the dishes with the most beautiful girl in the galaxy. I was worn out but agreed that Zav should start immediately. I kept seeing Cassie's drawing of the living room and it served as a stark reminder of the high cost of failure.

# THE STATION SEARCH

**Z**av worked with me for several hours after dinner, taking me through exercises designed to clear my mind and give me easy access to my empathic abilities. I thought I'd learned how to do this from my mother, but the methods she taught me were only the beginning. From my point of view, Zav's training was revolutionary. In just the few hours we worked together, I advanced farther than I'd managed working on my own since making my big psychic breakthrough outside of Pegasus Station.

By the time the four children went off to bed, I was exhausted. Still, I kept pushing Zav to teach me more and pushing myself to master his teaching as quickly as possible. The fourth time I refused Zav's suggestion to get some sleep, Michelle intervened.

"All right, babe, that's enough for tonight." Michelle took my hands and pulled me out of my chair. "You're barely able to keep your head up as it is."

"But I've got to be ready when the searchers come," I mumbled even as I rose to my feet.

"You won't do us any good if you're too worn out to think straight, much less use your powers," Michelle replied. "Besides, Zav needs sleep, too."

"Bless you, child." Zav's knees popped as he stood, providing an audible reminder that he was considerably older than me. "Michelle, did I overhear you making arrangements for a room and a bed?"

"Yes, Zav, and the kids cooperated fully. The girls are doubling up in Cassie's room and we're sleeping in Kristin's room." Michelle kissed Zav on the cheek. "Thank you for making us feel welcome and thank you for helping us."

Zav smiled gently at my wife. "Thank you for accepting my little family, oddities and all. Now scoot. I'm sure a young married couple can think of better things to do than listen to an old man blather on."

Michelle steered me into Kristin's room and helped me get ready for bed. I managed to find the strength to kiss Michelle goodnight before falling into a deep sleep.

I awoke to strange sounds—laughter and the clatter of pots and pans. Deciding to put my training to the test, I cleared my mind—easy to do so soon after waking up—and reached out with my ability. I picked up three people happily involved in something, one of them obviously Michelle. There were two others whose feelings were muddled as if something was interfering with my power. From my training the previous night, I realized I could determine the sex of the person generating the emotions. The other two happy ones were female so must be Cassie and Kristin. The muddled ones had to be Gene and Mark, with their telepathic abilities interfering with my incompatible empathic abilities. I didn't pick up anyone who might be Zav, so you can imagine my surprise when I found him sitting at his data pad when I came out.

Michelle met me with a quick kiss. "Good morning, sleepyhead."

Grinning mischievously, Cassie came up as Michelle returned to serving breakfast. She pulled my head down and kissed my cheek. "Good morning, sleepyhead."

My suspicions were aroused when a giggling Kristin followed

Cassie and confirmed when Gene and Mark, both smirking, approached after Kristin.

"If Zav tries to kiss me, I'm leaving," I announced with a laugh.

"Perish the thought, my boy," Zav commented. "Mind you, if we were all kissing *Michelle*, I believe I'd find a way to overcome my reticence."

Eying the plates of eggs, bacon, and waffles the kids were carrying to the table, I asked, "How long have you all been awake?"

"An hour or so," Michelle replied. "But you were so tired we decided to let you sleep late. Besides, you've got a busy day of training ahead of you and will need the extra sleep."

"She's right, Matt," Zav said. "Mentioning training, have you tried exercising your powers yet?"

I described what I picked up from the crowd and how easy it all had been for me. "But that brings up a really big question, Zav."

"You want to know why you couldn't read me." It wasn't a question, but Zav waited until I nodded before continuing, "I'm a psychic null—I have no powers nor can I be affected by any mental or emotional powers. Psi Corps actively searches for people like me to work as trainers because we won't fall prey to our charges' powers. Kristin's telekinesis can affect me because she could hurl something at me, but the rest of you have no more effect on me than Michelle does." Zav gave a wry grin, "Less, really, since Michelle is a lovely young woman."

Kristin and Cassie crossed their arms, canted their hips, and glared at Zav. Kristin demanded, "Aren't *we* lovely young women, too?"

"You are lovely *too-young* women," Zav replied.

The two girls exchanged glances, nodded at each other, and relaxed their stances. Cassie spoke for both of them. "Just as long as you recognize that we're lovely."

Settling down to breakfast, Michelle told me how Kristin uses her ability to sabotage scanners around the space station. In preparation for our arrival, she'd psychically pulled chips from sockets, loosened connections, and otherwise made sure no scanners were working anywhere near the route we took from the airlock to the apartment.

"If they hadn't done that, station security could have simply fed our images into recognition software and run it against the recordings from yesterday," Michelle said.

"Won't that spark suspicions and narrow down their search to this general area?" I asked. "I mean, how often do the scanners go out?"

"All the time," Kristin said, a grin lighting up her face. "Every day, I go out and sabotage scanners all over the station. Station authorities have run system checks, replaced equipment, and even brought in expensive experts to examine the system. For some reason, they never find anything to explain the failures."

Michelle bestowed a smile on our host. "Zav runs a tight ship. Daddy would approve."

"Wait," I said, "why can't Kristin sabotage a few sensors in the service tunnels during the search? Michelle and I can just hide there until the search moves on."

Michelle shook her head. "I already considered that, babe. Security sends out repair teams within an hour or two—much more quickly than the search of this area will take. Even if we evaded the search and got to the tunnels, a repair crew would come along and find us."

"Can't we just take Kristin with us and keep moving?" I asked.

Zav shook his head. "Residents are ordered to stay in their homes during a search. If Kristin isn't here when they reach us, it will trigger an alarm and a more intensive search until she's found."

From there, conversation tapered off as we busied ourselves eating. After breakfast, Zav and I returned to training. He worked me hard until we broke for lunch. After that, he suggested we run a few experiments.

I sat in Cassie's room and waited for Zav to send one of the three girls to the room to fetch something. My task was to absorb the curiosity for the search from whoever came down the hall. He sent them one at a time and each time I failed to do anything to dissuade them from finding whatever Zav asked them to find. He mixed up the rotation, sent two girls at once, and tried everything he could think of to spark my ability.

After an hour and a half of abject failure, I was irritable and tiring and very much afraid my failure would doom us all. From down the hall, I heard Zav quietly tell the others it was time to try something else.

"Michelle, go comfort Matt," Zav said. "I'm sure he's taking this harder than anyone else."

I sank deeper into misery and found myself thinking everyone else would be far better off if I simply wasn't here. In my dejection, I embraced that thought and let it envelope me. Michelle came into the room, concern written on her face. Then her concern changed to puzzlement. She looked around the room, shook her head, and left.

"Where's Matt?" Zav asked.

"Huh?" Michelle responded.

"I sent you to comfort Matt," Zav said. "Did he send you away?"

"I...didn't notice him," she replied, uncertainty creeping into her voice.

"You didn't notice your husband?"

Feet pounded down the hallway. As the three girls crowded into the room behind him, Zav asked, "Matt, what did you do?"

All three of the girls looked around and I realized their eyes just sort of slid past me. It was as if they tried to focus on me and then lost interest. Comprehension dawned on me and I gave a whoop. The girls all jumped, their eyes bugging out at me.

"How did you do that, babe?" Michelle asked, her startled expression transforming into an excited one.

"I just felt so depressed at my failure that I just sort of wished I wasn't here," I replied. "I guess I was broadcasting 'leave me alone' hard enough that you couldn't focus on me."

Michelle and Cassie hugged me at the same time and Cassie

said, "I knew you wouldn't let us all die in the living room. Bring on those searchers because you're ready for them."

I patted Cassie's head and said, "I wouldn't say I'm ready for the search team yet. I've only pulled this off once and that was by accident."

"Quite right, Matt," Zav said. "Now we have to see if you can do it on purpose. Ladies, let's go back down the hall and try again."

Michelle, Cassie, and Kristin left the room. As Zav turned to go, he added, "Remember, if you fail it will probably end up costing all of us our lives."

"Gee, that helps ever so much, Zav." My voice dripped with irritated sarcasm. "There's nothing like doubling down on the pressure to make a guy feel relaxed."

"Good, because it's evident your abilities work much better when you're overwhelmed with negative emotions." Zav looked down the hall after the retreating girls and a grin split his face. "Or, in certain cases involving Michelle, extremely positive emotions. But somehow I think it would be best if you and she were clothed and less...active...when the search team arrives."

I couldn't help laughing but quickly sobered again as Zav followed after the others. Over the next hour, he sent the girls down the hall in ones and twos. At first, success was fleeting. Sometimes I simply failed. Sometimes, I succeeded in making whoever came into the room look around in disinterest for a few seconds before my exultation at success ruined my concentration and they saw me. Still, my success rate increased and I found myself able to maintain the right frame of mind longer than a few seconds.

Zav called a welcome break and took the opportunity to send the boys out into the station to see what was going on. He also sent Kristin off on her daily sensor sabotage mission.

As the others cleared out, Michelle said to Cassie, "This is as good a time as any to clear off the walls in your room."

Zav's eyebrows shot up. "My God, I'd completely forgotten about that."

Cassie asked, "What's wrong with my walls?"

Michelle tousled Cassie's hair. "They're covered in sketches of the two people those search teams will be looking for, silly."

"Oh yeah," Cassie said. In a small voice, she asked, "We don't have to throw them away, do we? They're my first real connection with you and Da- Um, with you and Matt."

Michelle stared at Cassie for a second, an odd expression on her face, before asking, "Did you almost call Matt 'Dad'?"

Abashed, Cassie looked down at the floor and fidgeted as she answered, "I... That is... Well-"

Cassie's face clouded up and she dashed down the hall and slammed her bedroom door.

Zav shook his head in dismay. "I'm sorry, but I told you how heavy her emotional investment is with you two."

Michelle hugged me, blinking rapidly in an attempt to stem the flow of tears. Her emotions blazed brightly to my empathic ability though I'd have known what she was feeling even without my ability. Pulling her tight, I said, "Of course."

My wife leaned her head back and looked into my eyes. "Of course, *what*?"

"Sometimes emotions speak far more clearly than words, hon, and yours are shouting so loudly I don't even need empathic abilities to understand you." I kissed her gently. "Why don't you go tell Cassie?"

"We should tell her together," Michelle said.

"Cassie's emotions are fragile right now. It will be easier for her if just one of us goes down there." I turned her toward the hallway. "And who better to talk to her than the most beautiful girl in the galaxy?"

Michelle headed down the hall, her steps lightening as she went. She knocked gently on Cassie's door, exchanged a few quiet words through the door, then opened it and went inside. Looking back at Zav, I found him staring at me with incomprehension written all over his face.

"I fully trust you and Michelle will not purposefully do

anything to hurt Cassie," he said, "but please tell me what the two of you are planning."

"It wasn't clear?" I asked, surprised.

"Young man, I am neither an empath nor your wife," Zav declared. "Your exchange with Michelle might as well have been gibberish as far as I'm concerned."

"Oh, right. Sorry about that, Zav." I took a deep breath and said, "When all of this is over, Michelle and I are going to adopt Cassie. We'll adopt all four of the kids if the other three are willing."

Zav's mouth opened and closed several times as if he couldn't quite find the right words to express what he was feeling. Finally, he said, "My boy, you and Michelle are so young. Are you ready for the financial burden—?"

I ruined his speech by laughing out loud. "God above, Zav, I'm a billionaire. None of these kids could ever be a financial burden. And don't worry, we have more than enough room for a beloved uncle, too."

A high pitched shriek sounded from down the hall, followed by a wave of emotion so strong it briefly swamped my empathic senses. A few seconds later, Cassie's door flew open and the girl charged down the hall at me. Her brown eyes shone with tears and her brunette hair flew behind her as she ran. Realizing she wasn't slowing down, I braced myself and caught her as she leapt at me. Cassie's arms wrapped tightly around my neck and held on with such ferocity I wondered if she'd ever let go. Down the hall, Michelle leaned against the wall, her arms crossed and grinning at me.

I grinned back. "I take it Cassie was amenable to the idea?"

"Does *amenable* mean I want you to adopt me?" Cassie asked through her tears.

"It does."

"Then yeah, I'm amenable." She kissed my cheek then laid her head on my shoulder. "Am I too old to call you Daddy?"

"Honey, you can call me Daddy until you're a hundred and

three." Still carrying Cassie, I started down the hall toward Michelle. "Now, let's get your room cleaned up. We don't want company finding a messy room, do we?"

"No, Daddy," Cassie murmured.

We took our time clearing the walls, removing the drawings carefully so none of them tore. I sorted the drawings meticulously, making sure each timeline's drawings were arranged in chronological order, and then gathered the timeline stacks so they were also in the proper order. Michelle carefully stayed out of my way, sometimes shaking her head as she watched me. Cassie looked back and forth between the two of us, a bemused expression on her young face.

Finally, she turned to Michelle. Jerking her thumb in my direction, she asked, "What's his deal?"

"Your soon-to-be father can be very...particular...about how some things are arranged," Michelle replied.

"Ask your soon-to-be mother about organizing her blasters, power packs, and hand-to-hand weapons," I said. "And don't even get me started on arranging the furniture for optimal lines of fire."

"Those things you disparage could save your life someday," Michelle retorted.

"And my organization methods can save time, which means having more time to spend living life," I shot back.

"Wow, you two are so weird *I'm* going to seem like the normal one in the family!" Cassie exclaimed, her eyes dancing.

I put Cassie's drawings into a box and asked Zav where we could hide it. Telling us he had a place outside of the apartment which would be perfect, Zav took the box.

"Keep practicing while I'm gone, Matt," Zav said, then left.

I absolutely nailed my 'ignore me' broadcasts once we started up again. Perhaps the break helped me concentrate better or maybe it was the euphoria I felt about having Cassie join the family—I prefer crediting the latter—but Michelle and Cassie only noticed me when I wanted them to do so. After I remained unnoticed for five minutes while both of them were in the room,

Michelle declared me ready for the next step—keeping her hidden as well.

And that's where it all fell apart. No matter what I tried, I could not extend my power to cover Michelle. Time after time, Cassie came into the room and immediately focused on Michelle. Cassie couldn't see me standing right next to my wife, but Michelle was always right there. After thirty minutes of continuous failure, I was even having trouble masking my presence from Cassie.

I finally called a halt to it and, dejected, dropped onto Cassie's bed. Cassie and Michelle settled on either side of me, offering supportive hugs. I pulled them both close and whispered, "I'm sorry. You've put your faith in the wrong man."

Before Michelle or Cassie could offer hollow words in reply, we heard the apartment door open.

"Cassie?" Zav avoided calling my name or Michelle's, no doubt to ensure some sensor out in the corridor didn't record the words and trigger an alert with security.

"I'm in my room," Cassie replied.

Seconds later, Zav took in the look on my face. "You weren't able to reproduce that first success, Matt?"

"Just the opposite, actually," I said with a heavy sigh. "The problem is I can't expand it to include Michelle."

"Yeah, I couldn't see Daddy unless he let me," Cassie added. "But I saw Mom every time."

Michelle started, surprised but pleased at how naturally Cassie used her soon-to-be title. Zav nodded his understanding, scratched his chin absently, and stared off into nowhere.

"I thought this could be an issue," Zav said after half a minute. "I puzzled over it while finding a place to store Cassie's box and might have an answer—or the start of one."

"I'm all ears," I said, feeling a small spark of hope.

"Cassie, go down the hall and stay there until I call you," Zav instructed the girl.

Once Cassie was gone, Zav pointed toward one corner of the

room. In low tones, he said, "Michelle, wedge yourself into that corner as tightly as you can. Matt, you stand directly in front of her once she's in place. Block as much of her from view as possible."

Understanding dawned on both of us and we quickly positioned ourselves. Zav had me reposition myself slightly before declaring himself satisfied.

"Once you're ready, Matt, I'll call Cassie."

I closed my eyes for a few seconds, clearing my mind, and then nodded at Zav. As he called for the young precognitive, I projected disinterest. Zav kept his back to us, not turning around until Cassie entered the room. With bated breath, I waited for Cassie to come straight to Michelle. Instead, her gaze swept right past our corner of the room. My celebratory grin was just forming when Cassie's eyes swung back to our position. With some obvious force of will, she stared right at us.

"Are they in the corner, Zav?" she asked.

Deflated, I stopped broadcasting and Cassie's eyes focused fully on me. Stepping aside so Michelle could get out of the corner, I asked, "What did I do wrong?"

"Nothing," Cassie replied. "But I saw a little bit of Michelle's shirt. That blue she's wearing caught my attention."

"Good work, Cassie," Michelle said. "Now I'll know to wear a color that matches the wall."

"That should help," I said, "but I don't like the idea of just hanging out in the corner of the room. Can we both fit into one of the closets so a searcher won't simply trip over us?"

"Of course, Matt. This was just an experiment to see if this approach had any hope of working. Obviously, it does," Zav assured me.

We worked for a while longer with similar success. Then Zav had me try walking about the apartment while broadcasting disinterest. That was a complete failure on my part. I was a long way from walking and broadcasting at the same time and never managed to take even a single step without losing focus.

"It would have been handy to walk around the station invisible," I said, "but I'll settle for staying hidden from the search team when they arrive."

"You know you're not truly invisible even if people can't see you, right babe?" Michelle asked.

"What do you mean? That sounds just like being invisible to me," Cassie said.

"Matt's ability only works on a person's mind," Michelle replied.

"Yeah, I know *that*," Cassie rolled her eyes, giving us a mild taste of pubescent insolence.

Arching an eyebrow, Michelle crossed her arms. "And?"

"And what?" Cassie deflected.

"If you know how Matt's power works, tell me why he's not really invisible," Michelle sent the question right back to the girl.

A look of annoyance flashed briefly on Cassie's face, but that vanished as she considered the question properly. After a few seconds, her face cleared and she nodded. "Oh, I get it! People around Daddy might not see him, but sensors will. And so will anyone watching him on a camera."

"Exactly! I guess you *are* just that smart," Michelle said, bestowing a smile on Cassie.

The girl beamed and, just as the door opened to admit Gene and Mark, said, "Thanks, Mom."

The two boys just stared at Cassie, leaving the door open behind them. Several people walked past the door, casually glancing inside in the incurious way people tend to do. Zav quickly stepped in between Michelle and the door. Taking a cue from him, I turned my back to the door.

"Boys, how many times must I tell you to close the door," Zav said in a loud and stern voice.

A knowing laugh sounded from outside as Gene jumped to obey. We didn't relax until it slid completely shut.

Anger lacing his voice, Zav said, "You both know an alert is out for Matt and Michelle, yet you just left the door wide open so any passerby could see them. Explain yourselves."

"We were surprised when Cassie called Michelle 'Mom'," Gene said with a shrug. "Why did she do that?"

Unable to contain herself, Cassie blurted, "Because they're going to adopt all of us when we get away from here."

The two boys stared at Cassie for a second and then transferred their gazes to us. Finally, Gene turned to Zav and asked, "What do you think about this, Zav?"

"Matt has made it very clear that I'm welcome, too. And I must say it will be much easier keeping you four safe with the resources available to one of the richest families on Draconis."

Mark's eyes widened. "Do you mean Matt really is as rich as Cassie says?"

Zav's eyebrows drew down. "Obviously you never read those news stories I told you to read, Mark." He shifted his glare to Gene. "Did *you* read them?"

"I skimmed them," Gene replied. "So, if Matt and Michelle adopt us, does that mean I can get a hot car?"

"Tell you what," Michelle said, "let's get out of this first."

Gene shrugged acceptance. "Man, this is going to blow Kristin's mind."

"What about my mind?" Kristin asked, stepping through the apartment door just as Gene finished speaking. Unlike the boys, she quickly closed the door behind her.

Almost in unison, Cassie, Mark, and Gene told Kristin the adoption news. Zav added his blessing for the idea, answering Kristin's first question before she asked it.

Kristin processed the idea for a few seconds before asking, "I can still be me after the adoption, right? We don't have to become stuffy rich kids or anything? I don't have to go to a debutante ball, do I?"

Michelle passed that question to me, saying, "Heck if I know. I married into money but didn't grow up with it. Care to take her question, Matt?"

"Have I acted like a stuffy rich kid?" I asked.

Kristin grinned, "Nah, you're pretty tolerable."

"Now that we've settled *that* pressing question," Zav interjected, "perhaps Gene and Mark will deign to tell us what they discovered?"

Gene grimaced. "The station already has guards around our sector. They're letting people in, but no one can go out."

Zav nodded, checking his watch. "I assume that means they'll begin the search first thing tomorrow morning?"

"At seven," Mark confirmed. He looked carefully at Zav, Michelle, and me. "You don't look real scared—does that mean we're not all going to die?"

Cassie jumped in with an account of my progress. By the time she finished her story, the others wore hopeful smiles. Kristin offered her closet for our hiding place, but Gene had a more compelling idea.

"Use Mark's closet. He hardly ever hangs anything up, so there's plenty of stuff Michelle can hide under. That should make it easier for Matt." Gene flashed an evil grin. "If we toss Mark's unwashed socks in there, it'll be even easier to convince the searcher to go away."

Kristin joined in the fun. "But the stench might kill Matt and Michelle."

Michelle and I laughed, breaking off when we realized the others were seriously considering the socks might kill us. Looking to Zav, Michelle asked, "They aren't really *that* bad, are they?"

"Of course not," Zav said. Then he added, "You'll probably want to burn your clothes afterward, though."

Everyone laughed at that except Mark, Michelle, and me. Then it was time to fix dinner and formulate plans for the next morning. Tired from the stress of waiting and from my mental exertions during the day, I was ready for sleep earlier than normal. Michelle came to bed with me but had ideas other than sleep. Properly motivated, I had no trouble staying awake a while longer.

All of us except Cassie were up early the next morning. We set up Michelle's burrow under Mark's clothes and discovered Zav and Gene weren't kidding about Mark's socks. As Cassie slept on, Zav got a pensive look and glanced at her door often.

"What's on your mind, Zav? Why do you keep looking toward Cassie's room?" I asked.

"When Cassie sleeps this deeply, it usually means she's seeing a potential future."

That was definitely unsettling news, especially when seven came and went. The search was on and our precog was out. What was she seeing? Would her vision bear on our situation? Could it guide our actions? Would we receive any warnings in time to act on them?

A few minutes later, we got the answer to my last question. A fist pounded on the apartment door. A loud voice called, "In the name of the Federation, you are ordered to open the door and submit to a search of the premises."

Michelle and I hurried down the hall toward Mark's room. Just as we reached the door, Cassie dashed out of her room.

"They're already here? Why didn't you wake me up?" Before anyone could respond, she caught Michelle's hand. "If anything happens to us, you can find help in the loading bay on deck eighty-four."

Surprised, Michelle only managed a quick nod to Cassie before I hurried her through Mark's door and into his closet. She caught Cassie's gaze just before I pulled the closet door shut and whispered, "I love you, Cassie."

Zav opened the door as I hurried to hide Michelle among the smelly clothes littering the closet floor. I feared Zav would try to stall the search team and get himself hurt in the process. Fortunately, he was much smarter than that.

"Is this everyone who lives here?" an officious voice demanded loudly enough to carry through walls and doors easily.

"Yes, sir." Zav's much quieter voice barely made it to us. "Do you want us all to stay out here in the living room?"

The officious voice backed off a bit when he realized Zav was cooperating. "Yes, please. How many rooms are there besides this one?"

"Five, sir," Mark piped up, his voice perky and helpful. "That doesn't include the bathroom, but you probably don't want to look in there."

"Why not?" The voice held simple curiosity rather than the suspicion such a comment might normally arouse. Mark was obviously using his psychic ability to charm the team and, I hoped, dull any zeal they might have for the search.

"We've got *girls* using it and they've got so much stuff it's ridiculous. It's gross and it smells."

"It smells all right," Kristin sounded just like she was having a snit fit, "but that's because you and Gene stink."

With Michelle finally hidden in a corner, I stood before her and cleared my mind. It took a lot of effort, but I shut out the voices from the living room and carefully drew forth feelings of isolation and the desire to be left alone.

Distantly, I heard many feet coming down the hallway as the team spread out to perform their search. One pair of feet veered into Mark's room and I threw all of my concentration into projecting my 'go away and leave me alone' feelings.

I can't say how long I stood in the corner of the closet before the door opened. It couldn't have been very long, but keeping my full concentration on projecting emotions really screwed up my time sense. A man close to my own age stared into the closet, his eyes sweeping over the piles of clothes. His nose wrinkled as the smell of Mark's socks hit him.

"Damn, the girl really was right about the smell," he muttered, kicking at the clothes closest to the door. His gaze swept around the closet, passing right over me before concentrating on the floor. Waving his hand in front of his nose, the man backed out of the closet and shut the door.

I carefully checked the surge of elation I felt as darkness closed over us again and kept projecting emotions as the man poked around for a little longer.

"Hey Sarge?" a voice called from one of the other rooms. "Come look at this."

A set of heavy footsteps marched down the hall. The man searching Mark's room headed toward the voice, as well. A low-voiced conversation took place and then the whole search team returned to the living room.

"Sir, could you explain this?" The sergeant's tone was officious once again.

A few seconds passed, then Zav said, "It's just a drawing my youngest did. She's quite good, don't you think?"

"Real good," the sergeant agreed. "Would you care to tell me why she's drawn herself holding hands with the two people we're searching for?"

Oh, hell! How had we missed one of Cassie's drawings of Michelle and me? We cleared the walls entirely, but we *only* cleared the walls. Where else would Cassie have a drawing, though? Then it hit me—we never looked in her sketchbook.

"Cassie, can you answer the man's question?" Zav asked.

Cassie replied, sounding on the verge of tears. "I... I j-just saw their pictures on the vid and they looked so nice and all..."

"There you have it, Sergeant," Zav said. "It can't be too surprising that an artistically inclined girl took her inspiration from the images you've been broadcasting."

"If that's the case, sir," the Sergeant responded, his voice stern, "why didn't she draw them in the clothing they were wearing in those images?"

For the first time, Zav's voice took on an edge of exasperation. "Do you have *any* experience with females, Sergeant? Many of them, especially ones Cassie's age, are quite fascinated with clothes. So what if she drew different clothing?"

"That's a pretty good argument, sir," the Sergeant replied. "But station security found a brief image of the couple as they passed through one of the shopping districts. Can you explain how your girl just *happened* to draw them in the clothes they were wearing at the time?"

"Perhaps she saw them in the shopping district and subconsciously remembered what they were wearing," Zav suggested.

"That could be," the sergeant allowed, "but until we can get to the bottom of this I'm going to have to take all of you to station security."

"I *must* protest, Sergeant!" Zav said with vehemence. "We have rights, damn you."

"Not with the station under martial law, you don't," the sergeant snarled. "Now, are you going to come along quietly or will you force my men to be rough?"

"We'll go quietly," Zav sighed, defeat evident in his tone. "Come along, children."

I heard the apartment door slide open and, several seconds later, slide shut again.

Clothing stirred as Michelle sat up. "Dear God, Matt, if station security follows normal intake procedure, it won't take long for them to discover who Zav and the kids really are."

"I know." I pulled Michelle to her feet and opened the door. "This must be what Cassie saw in her dreams."

"So we wait for the search to end and then go to the loading bay on deck eighty-four?" Michelle asked.

"I don't have a better idea right now," I said. "Besides, we're going to need all the help we can get if we're going to rescue Zav and the kids."

Left to myself, I'd have spent too much time worrying about our friends and too little time preparing for the moment when we left the apartment. Fortunately, Jonas trained his daughter far better than that.

"Let's see what clothing options we've got for you, Matt," Michelle said in response to my rescue declaration.

Distracted by the first stages of worry, my wife's statement didn't really register. "What?"

"Clothes, Matt. You heard that sergeant—they have a brief vid shot of us crossing that shopping district when we first came onto the station." She plucked at my shirt. "The recognition software in the sensors will pick us out in a matter of seconds if we go out wearing these clothes."

"Right. Good idea, Michelle. I'm too big to wear Gene's or Mark's clothes," I replied, starting down the hall. "Let's see what Zav's got. What about you?"

"We already know I can wear Kristin's clothes. Her shirts are a bit tight in the chest, but that will just ensure guys don't spend much time looking at my face."

I could not think of a response to that line—Lord knows she was right—so I just left it alone. "What about hair color and things like that?"

"We're kind of limited in what's available in the apartment," Michelle said, "but there's enough for me to work with."

My father would have approved of Zav's wardrobe. It was much too staid for my tastes, but Michelle liked the options. She selected a conservatively cut suit which fit reasonably well when worn over my own clothes. I recognized the value of having the option to change my appearance somewhat by simply peeling off a shirt or pair of pants, but that didn't make the double layers any more comfortable.

Michelle selected a stylish skirt and blouse. As promised, the blouse emphasized her breasts. The skirt showed Michelle's legs to good effect and shifted enticingly with the swing of her hips. She selected more sensible shoes though also stayed away from entirely flat heels, ensuring a change in her height.

Next, she went to work on me with makeup and improvised hair coloring. "We're going to age you a bit, babe. A little gray in the temples, a little shadow added to some of your laugh lines, and you'll look like a forty-year-old."

Once she finished with me, Michelle colored her own hair and eyebrows red. Next, she did...something...with eye liner, a lash brush, rouge, and lipstick. When she was done, she looked a few years older than her actual age of twenty-one and considerably more sexually available. She watched my reaction with a sly, sophisticated smile.

"When all of this is over, do you want me to do myself up like this for you one night?" she asked.

"It's a nice package, hon, but if I wanted to score with someone like Jayna I'd have done it back in high school." Michelle's eyebrows rose in surprise, so I added, "You look really hot, but it's like the makeup is designed to hide something—like you don't really care about me beyond getting another notch on your bedpost. You know, the lay 'em and leave 'em type of girl mothers always warned their sons about."

"Huh," Michelle said, obviously surprised at my reaction.

"Rich guys have hot girls throwing themselves at them so often it actually gets boring. I never wanted that kind of thing, Michelle. I wanted a woman who would stay with me forever, one who was even more beautiful on the inside than she was on the outside. That's why I held out for you."

"Dammit, Matt, don't you know you're not supposed to make a girl cry right after she puts on makeup?" Michelle blinked her eyes rapidly. "I was expecting a simple 'Hell, yeah, baby' from you. What made you get all serious?"

I shrugged. "What we're about to do is dangerous, hon. If we fail, the *best* result we can hope for is that Psi Corps takes me away from you forever. I don't want you ever doubting just how important you are to me."

"Then we'd better make damn sure we don't fail, babe," Michelle said with vehemence.

Half an hour later, station security gave the all clear for our sector, releasing the occupants to go about their day. Michelle and I waited another thirty minutes, giving time for normal traffic patterns to form, and then headed for the loading bay on level eighty-four.

The recognition software was looking for a couple, so Michelle and I kept our distance from each other. That was really nerve-wracking—if anything went wrong, neither of us could reach the other in time to help. It was equally difficult watching men of all ages surreptitiously watching my wife stride confidently down corridors and through shopping and office districts.

Some of the men looking at her made no attempt to hide their interest, and one even tried chatting her up. Michelle laughed at something he said, touched his arm in a way which promised intimacy might be in the cards later, and made an entry in her pad. She waggled her fingers enticingly as she walked away and even added a bit more swing to her hips. The guy bumped forearms with a companion and walked away grinning widely. Even knowing Michelle was acting, it wasn't an easy scene to watch. On the other hand, it was certain Michelle wasn't acting like your typical fugitive.

Eventually, I reached an elevator which could take me to the loading bay on level eighty-four. Trying to appear casual, I hoped for a slow-arriving elevator as I waited for Michelle to catch up. That meant the elevator arrived within seconds. I shuffled slowly toward the car. It filled up quickly, giving me a brief hope that I'd have to wait for the next elevator. Unfortunately, there was room for me when I reached the door. Looking over my shoulder as I entered the car, I saw Michelle hurrying to catch the elevator. I stabbed a finger onto the Door Open button, drawing a few irritated looks from other passengers. Then Michelle, announced by the enticing aroma of perfume, wedged her way into the car.

The irritation on the faces of the men faded quickly though the other women in the elevator were less forgiving. Michelle breathlessly thanked whoever held the elevator for her and a man older than Jonas—one who couldn't even *reach* the button—took credit by saying, "You're most welcome, young lady."

Michelle flashed a bright smile at him and spent the short elevator ride chatting amiably about nothing much with the men crowded around her. I listened to the other conversations and heard two men discussing the lock-down in Zav's sector and the news that the search teams had found the people they were looking for.

"It seems like a lot of trouble to put everyone through just to find some psychic," one man said. "Whoever they are, they're obviously not hurting anyone."

"They abandoned a spaceship running at high speed when they were close to the station," the second man replied. "That was incredibly dangerous."

"It wasn't really that dangerous. There's a hell of a lot more empty space than there is occupied space—even this close to the station," the first man said. "I spent twenty years in the navy and can promise you the odds of them hitting anything were pretty low. Besides, they wouldn't have tried that if the Feds weren't after them."

"Maybe so, but do you want unregulated psychics wandering around free to use their powers on us?" the other countered.

The first dismissed this claim with a wave of his hand. "Do you honestly think Psi Corps finds anything close to all of the psychics out there? I read that something like one out of every few thousand people has some latent psychic abilities. In the Terran Federation alone, that's tens of millions of psychics of one kind or another. They're not bothering me, so why should we bother them?"

The conversation drifted off into sports scores after that, but I found myself heartened by it. Perhaps the citizens of the Federation were open to changing the laws concerning psychics.

Our elevator finally reached level eighty-four and Michelle and I got off. Once again, we kept our distance as we wandered through the loading bay. Michelle didn't stand out as badly as she had back on Rockport Station, but she still drew more than a few stares from the men working in the bay—and more than a few glares from the women working alongside the men. This time, though, I had little trouble ignoring the looks she drew since I kept my eyes roving over the faces of the people in the loading bay.

The loading bay was huge, so it took me forty minutes to wend my way through the crowds and traverse it from one end to another. A couple of hundred meters from the back end of the docking bay—the place where smaller ships docked and the crowd was considerably thinner—I finally spotted a familiar face. The sight surprised me so much I simply stopped walking and stared openly for a few seconds. Rousing myself, I looked toward Michelle who was thirty meters away and watching me closely.

Our eyes met and I jerked my head toward the familiar face. Better prepared and far better trained at hiding reactions than I am, Michelle simply nodded when she spotted the face. With a smile, Michelle started working her walk and drew a lot of looks. With so much attention directed at her, I had no trouble stealing up behind the oh-so-familiar man.

Stopping next to him, I spoke quietly. "You know, in most cultures it's wrong for a man to openly leer at his nephew's wife."

The man looked at me for the first time, his eyes going wide in surprised recognition.

I met his gaze impassively and said, "Hello, Uncle Gunther."

# THE PLAN

Give credit to my uncle, he recovered quickly. "I'm impressed you found me, Matt. I'm even more impressed you've managed to evade the navy search teams who've been combing the station for you and your lovely wife."

"I could say the same about you," I responded. Then, because I was still really pissed off at him for all the years he kept my parents prisoner in his hidden pirate base, I added, "Except for the wife bit, of course. That didn't work out so well for you."

Gunther's expression hardened at my gibe. Michelle immediately started our way, her eyes going cold even as she still worked her hips. Gunther saw her, as well, and let his features soften. It didn't stop Michelle, but it did slow down her advance.

"I'm surprised you went for such a low blow. You never were a cruel child growing up," my uncle said to me as he shook his head as if in sorrow. "I'm disappointed in you, lad."

"Said the kidnapper uncle to the nephew he all but orphaned." It was my turn for a set jaw and steely eyes. Seeing that, Michelle quickened her pace again. I shook my head in disgust. "Your disappointment in me pales in comparison to the vast, yawning cavern of disgust I feel for you."

Gunther leaned toward me, anger flaring to life in his eyes. Just as he opened his mouth to let me have it, Michelle grabbed both of us around the neck and pretended to hug us. When she'd pulled us close, Michelle hissed, "Are the two of you *trying* to draw station security's attention? In case you've forgotten, the Feds are hunting both of you."

Michelle gave us both one of those near-the-cheek false kisses exchanged by women the galaxy over. She smiled brightly at the two of us and said, "Dearest Uncle, is there someplace private where we can talk?"

"Of course, child," Gunther responded in kind. "Why don't you come aboard my ship?"

I didn't say 'oh hell no' but my face must have telegraphed it to my uncle. "I'm no longer with my old shipping firm, lad. These days, all I've got is a small freighter with a small crew—just me, in fact."

Michelle and I exchanged a glance. She arched her eyebrows, essentially asking if we should trust Gunther. I gave him a quick surface check with my ability and felt no deception in Gunther. I shrugged and nodded. "Lead on, Uncle."

Michelle linked arms with Gunther—ensuring he couldn't just bolt away from us—and filled the air with inane chatter about shoes, fashion, shopping, and how I refused to let her spend *any* money without Gunther's approval. For a woman who abhorred small talk, Michelle was very good at faking it.

A few minutes of walking brought us to a small docking bay in which a smaller-than-expected freighter sat. Gunther coded open the hatch and we all entered the ship. I'd like to say I felt better hidden from Piscain Station's sensors, but I'd just traded one source of stress for another.

"How about a tour of the ship, Uncle-by-marriage?" Michelle asked as soon as the hatch slid shut again. "We can start at the front of the ship and work our way backwards in a very careful and systematic way."

Despite himself, Gunther gave a brief smile. "Your father

taught you well, young lady. I must say, I was rather relieved when I read you and Matt got married. He's a smart and talented young man, but he always had his head in the clouds. Matt needs someone practical to keep him pointed in the right direction."

"Have you ever considered what it must have been like for my husband after you kidnapped his parents?" Michelle asked icily. "Can you imagine *knowing* your parents are alive but being unable to tell anyone *why* you know that or convince anyone to even give a damn?"

"No, I never thought of it that way," my uncle admitted. "Matt has found quite an adamant defender in you, Michelle."

"Damned right he has."

"No doubt you'd do anything for him, too," Gunther said, showing us into the cargo compartment and completing his tour of the ship. "Even break the law."

"I see where you're going with this, Gunther, and it's a false equivalence," Michelle admonished. "You kidnapping Matt's parents is not the same as me helping Matt avoid capture by Psi Corps."

"Federation law says otherwise, Michelle," Gunther replied, crossing his arms. "But let's be honest with each other. If you thought it was in Matt's best interests to shove me out an airlock, I'd be breathing vacuum right now."

"If I thought it was in my best interests, maybe I'd help her do it," I interrupted the discussion. "But let's cut to the chase—are you trying to blame my parents' kidnapping on Aunt Tess while casting yourself as the reluctant-but-supportive husband?"

"Yes, because it's true." Seeing the skeptical looks on our faces, Gunther continued, "I was born into piracy and had my whole career path laid out in front of me. I never enjoyed the life and was always looking for a way out of it. I thought I'd found that way out when your aunt and I fell in love, figuring the Brotherhood couldn't touch a Connaught son-in-law. I didn't count on Tess loving my career more than she loved me."

"And you expect me to believe that?" Even as I asked the question, I remembered my last conversation with Aunt Tess and her willingness to sacrifice me if I gave her too much trouble.

"You already do believe me, Matt," Gunther said, "but why stop with mere belief? You're supposed to be a psychic—use your powers and see if I'm being honest."

"I think you should do it, babe," Michelle said. "The sooner we know if we can trust your uncle, the better."

After all of my recent training and experience, it didn't take me very long. I sifted through his deepest emotions, verifying his truthfulness and discovering one other thing. "After everything she's put you through, you still love Aunt Tess?"

"Of course I do. Love isn't rational and it's not something you can turn on and off like a light." Gunther smiled ruefully and gestured all around him. "This ship is perfect for smuggling, which I'm doing to raise money. Once I have enough ready cash, I can bribe her way out of prison."

Michelle considered this. "Tess doesn't strike me as a 'life on the run' type of woman. Are you sure she'll thank you?"

"Life on the run must be better than life in prison," Gunther countered. "Even if she leaves me, I'll have the satisfaction of knowing she's free."

Michelle and I exchanged calculating glances, then I asked, "How much money do you need, Gunther?"

"Tess is a high-profile prisoner. I'll need at least fifty million credits."

I smiled for the first time. "If you help us rescue our friends from station security and get somewhere safe, I'll pay you sixty million."

Gunther barked a laugh. "Do you expect me to believe you're on the run and have that kind of money?"

"Do you really believe my father and Jonas wouldn't stock an escape ship with everything Michelle and I would need to get away, including money?" I countered.

That brought him up short. "Show me."

I pulled out the credit sticks I'd taken with us when we left our spaceship and thumbed the balance displays. Gunther gave the numbers a quick look and asked, "What do you want me to do and when do we start?"

"We get started on the rescue right now," I reply to my uncle, "but I have no idea what I need you to do."

Uncle Gunther's eyes narrowed. "You don't have a plan? Why the hell did you come to me, then?"

"I came to you because a twelve-year-old girl told me to," I said. "I didn't even know I needed help until four hours ago."

Gunther nodded as if he comprehended the situation. He leaned against a bulkhead, folded his arms, and asked, "So what happened? Did these friends of yours get caught stealing from a shopkeeper?"

"You saw the kind of money we've got. Do you really think a friend of mine would have to steal? More, do you honestly think I'd pay you sixty million credits to break my friends out when they only faced a fine of a few hundred credits?" My uncle shrugged, conceding my point, so I continued, "Our friends are rogue psychics who have been on the run from Psi Corps for five or six years."

That shocked Gunther out of his studied uncaring pose. "God in heaven, boy, are you out of your mind? Those friends of yours are already in the Psi Corps office on the station by now. That's a whole different level of trouble you're talking about."

Michelle snorted in derision. "Yes, it's a dangerous situation. No, we don't have a rescue plan. Yes, we have to act very fast. All of this should have been obvious when Matt offered you sixty million credits to help us."

"Psi Corps has an office on the station?" I asked.

"Yes, and it's a big one with quite a few psychics assigned to it," Gunther replied. "Psi Corps likes it on the Piscain Hub for the same reason shipping firms like it here—they can easily send psychics in a dozen different directions with minimal fuss."

"Why weren't those psychics assigned to the search teams?" I asked. All it would have taken was a telepath or maybe another empath joining the search team and they'd have found Michelle and me easily.

Gunther actually laughed in response to my question. "For one of the oldest reasons known to man—inter-service rivalry. You crossed the navy first, so they got first shot at capturing you. They'd no more have asked Psi Corps for help than they would ask a pirate gang. And if your friends are as high-profile as you say they are, you can bet the naval brass will lord their discovery over Psi Corps for years to come. And you can bet Psi Corps administrators will be scrambling to explain how those rogue psychics could stay hidden in the same space station as one of their larger offices."

"Thank God for small favors, I guess," Michelle murmured. "But our rescue just got a lot harder."

"Why even bother with the rescue?" Gunther asked. "Chances are the navy will be happy with their find. Sure, they'll go through the motions of searching the rest of the station, but they've successfully deflected embarrassing attention from them and onto Psi Corps, but all you have to do is wait for them to lift the travel restrictions. I'll take you out of here myself, once I'm free to leave."

"Unlike your old pirate gang, Michelle and I don't leave our friends behind just so we can get away safely," I said, a hint of a sneer slipping into my tone.

"Really, lad? And have you asked the love of your life what she thinks about that?" Gunther drawled.

"He doesn't have to ask me," Michelle said. "Our friends risked everything to help us. There is no way in hell we're going to abandon them when they need our help in return."

"That's very noble of you both," Gunther replied, "but you still don't have a plan and don't have much time to come up with one."

"I don't know, we're in better shape than Michelle and I were when we set off to rescue my parents," I said. "Then we only knew they were alive somewhere in the galaxy. Hell, we don't even have to search Piscain Station to find our friends. And even when we found my parents and your hidden pirate base, we didn't have a plan. We just made it up as we went along."

"But if outside help hadn't shown up, you'd have been captured or killed by those same pirates," my uncle countered. "No one on Piscain Station is going to lift a finger to help you."

Michelle and I exchanged looks and it didn't take my empathic powers to read her resignation. I nodded in agreement and the two of us turned away from Gunther and headed up the corridor toward the airlock.

"I trust you won't turn us in, Uncle," I called over my shoulder, "because we'll return the favor if we're picked up. Leave us alone and we'll leave you alone."

"And just where do you think you're going, young man?" Gunther demanded.

I didn't even bother turning around. "That worked when I was a minor living with you, but it won't work now."

"We're not going to concoct some hare-brained scheme to rescue your friends?" Gunther asked.

Michelle fielded this question. "You've made your position very clear. We won't trouble you again."

"You've got it wrong. I've gotten you to make your position very clear," Gunther said. "I don't have psychic powers and must rely on words and wit to learn these things. And you have convinced me that you are definitely going through with this rescue attempt."

I stopped and turned back to face my uncle. "Are you saying you were simply testing our resolve with your negative attitude?"

"Yes."

"And you're telling us you're actually willing to help us?"

"Yes—though I still want the sixty million credits." My uncle tilted his head slightly. "Couldn't you read that with those amazing psychic powers?"

"I could, but I didn't. Everyone deserves privacy in their own mind."

"You truly are an exceptional young man, Matt." Gunther smiled sheepishly, "Perhaps I have no reason to lay claim to pride, but I am quite proud of the man you've become." His sheepish smile transformed into a grin. "Also, while we were talking I had an idea or two for rescuing your friends."

We spent the next hour discussing and refining my uncle's idea. The idea was straight-forward—sound a decompression warning throughout the station and take advantage of the confusion to rescue Zav and the kids. Simple as the plan sounded, we had to figure out a lot of details before giving it a go.

I settled down in front of Gunther's data pad to exercise my hacking skills. Gunther headed out to utilize his connections with the station underworld. He carried a credit stick with a comparatively small balance of a few hundred thousand credits, more than enough to hire help and purchase supplies. Michelle plotted sensor readings for the naval ships in the system, intent on finding the least dangerous route to a wormhole.

I tackled station security first since the plan fell apart if I couldn't trigger the station's breach warnings. Without the benefit of the backdoors I'd used when hacking the GenCo systems on Pegasus Station, I had to rely entirely on my wits. Fortunately, Jonas hadn't let me rest on my laurels after we rescued Mom and Dad from the pirates. He drilled me all the harder, ensuring none of the systems I tried hacking had any connection to the GenCo system. He also brought in some very good network security experts to refine my existing skills and teach me new ones.

It took close to two hours for me to crack station security. I would have spent even more time working on it if one of the guys Jonas brought in hadn't taught me about social engineering and masking comm codes. Adopting the persona of a harried naval ensign, I called an equally harried departmental assistant administrator in station security. My carefully spun story about synchronizing search team work shifts and our inability to connect to security's shift roster yielded the assistant's password to the time-keeping system. While giving me his password, the guy even said, "What the hell, it's just the shift scheduling system."

If the guy had any idea what I could do with *any* admin level password into their system, he'd have hung up on me immediately. But most people really don't know how much damage a good hacker can do once they have access to the system. Rearranging the duty roster and changing schedules was just the beginning. I wanted to add Michelle and me to the navy security team roster, but in the end decided that was just too risky. Finally, I used the assistant's password as a stepping stone to far greater system access.

All of this took a lot of time. Gunther returned with purchases, checked on my progress, and then went out again with an expanded list of skills we needed to pull off our plan. Michelle brought lunch to me at some point and even stood over me until I ate it. It took longer than I hoped, but I finally found information on our friends. As we'd feared, once station security made a close inspection of the false identities Zav established for the five of them, everything fell apart quickly. Within an hour, security established their true identities and alerted Psi Corps.

The Psi Corps office immediately restricted the information at the highest level of classification and did their best to keep the findings out of navy hands. That would have worked if not for the admiral on hand for the naval maneuvers which were underway when Michelle and I entered the Piscain system. The flag officer outranked the local Psi Corps office chief and, despite having been in the system for only a week or so, had better relations with station security.

Reading between the lines, I got the idea homeless bums living in repair tunnels had a better relationship with station security than Psi Corps had. And that level of friction helped us out a bit. The admiral offered to transport our friends to the nearest full Psi

Corps facility in a fast courier under his command. The Psi Corps office chief, peeved he wasn't able to contain the embarrassing revelation that Zav and the kids were living right under his nose, tried commandeering the fast courier from the navy. By the time the inter-service pissing contest was over, the admiral had trampled all over the hapless station chief, promising he'd let a Psi Corps message drone exit the system once he was certain the emergency situation was well enough contained to resume external communication with the rest of the Federation. The station chief tried launching a drone anyway, but the navy intercepted and destroyed it.

Reading the station security summary reminded me of reading the minutes of some of the GenCo board's more contentious meetings. I'd seen preschoolers in mid-tantrum who were more reasonable than these high-ranking government officials. I relayed all of this to Michelle and we marveled at the behavior of these supposed adults. We also breathed sighs of relief. Our timetable was still tight, but not as tight as we had feared.

Finally, I turned my attention to Psi Corps. I didn't even consider trying social engineering with Psi Corps. God only knew what kind of psychics they had in the office watching out for that kind of thing. I was hardly what you'd call an expert on the subject and had no idea if it was even possible to set up a psychic firewall against that sort of thing, but I refused to jeopardize the entire rescue operation to make my job a little easier. Besides, I just needed access to Psi Corps' office procedures in case of station-wide emergencies. When the decompression alarm sounded, would they lock the office down or evacuate or do something else entirely different? Of course, the Psi Corps response was best summed up as 'it depends on the situation'—not nearly as useful as I'd hoped for. Essentially, the response was whatever the station chief decided it should be. It was not a particularly helpful policy from my point of view though I'm sure the station chief loved it.

My groan of frustration brought Michelle over to me. "Your

shoulders are hard as a rock, babe," she said as her hands began kneading my tense muscles. "You need to take a break."

"I'll take a break when our friends are with us on this ship and we're waving goodbye to the Piscain Hub." Despite my words, I leaned back in the chair and let myself enjoy the shoulder massage. I even tilted my head back just in case Michelle felt like giving me a quick kiss.

She did feel like it though it wasn't quick at all. Despite the situation—or maybe because of it—our kiss quickly turned passionate. Michelle's hands wandered down from my shoulders and caressed my chest. My hands rose and returned the favor though I think I got a lot more out of caressing Michelle's chest than she got caressing mine. Spinning around in the chair, I pulled Michelle into my lap and resumed our kiss.

"I suppose I should have known better than to leave young, horny newlyweds alone for so long." Uncle Gunther's voice startled us both though we didn't jump apart like I think he hoped we would. "You know, children, we've got a deadline for rescuing your friends."

Michelle spun the chair around so we both faced my uncle. "The deadline isn't quite as pressing as we thought, Gunther. Besides, Matt and I were just taking a short break."

"I remember being young and newly married, Michelle, and I saw where my nephew's hands were headed. If they'd gotten there and he managed to stop short of bedding you, he'd be a stronger man than I was at his age." A lascivious grin crossed my uncle's face. "And if you'd let him get that far without bedding him... Let's just say you never struck me as the teasing type."

"Here's an idea," I said, "let's stop talking about our sex life, Uncle, and start talking about what you've been doing for the last five hours."

"Well, I can promise you it's not been as interesting as what you were just doing, Matt," In response to my glare, Uncle Gunther raised his hands in a placating manner. "Okay, I'll drop that subject."

"Good," Michelle and I both said.

"I've managed to hire a collection of people with negotiable morals to help us with our distraction. One of them offered unexpected services." Uncle Gunther's expression turned serious. "How much more effective will our decompression alarm be if it's accompanied by an actual decompression?"

Uncle Gunther wanted to cause an actual decompression? Unbidden, images from school training vids came to mind—terrified people screaming wordlessly as they were sucked out into space to certain death. My head was shaking before I finally found my voice.

"Absolutely not!" The vehemence in my voice took my uncle aback. "We will not kill innocent people just to make our diversion more believable."

"I'm entirely with Matt on this," Michelle added, her tone equally forceful. "How could you even think we'd agree to something like that?"

"I'm not planning on killing anyone," Gunther said once we gave him a chance to respond. "The man who suggested the idea makes quite a good living from insurance settlements for 'accidents' he stages. He's pulled off decompression routines a dozen times all around the Federation and hasn't lost anyone yet. I don't know how he does this sort of thing, but his cons feature real holes in carefully secured areas, ensuring only his people get sucked out into space. He says he has teams waiting outside in spacesuits and the people playing the victim have vacuum harnesses worn under their clothes."

Michelle and I exchanged glances. I shrugged and she said, "An actual hole in the station with people tumbling through it would really help convince people there was cause for alarm."

"It might distract the navy, too," I suggested. "Lord knows we'll need all the help we can get escaping to a wormhole."

"I thought you'd like it," Uncle Gunther said. "And I'd like to add how deeply wounded I am that you thought I'd kill innocent people simply as a diversion."

"Said the ex-pirate and kidnapper of my parents-in-law," Michelle replied.

"Kidnapper, *not* murderer," Gunther growled in response.

Michelle inclined her head slightly, "That's a fair point. I apologize for suggesting you would cross that not-so-fine line."

Gunther actually clicked his heels and bowed slightly. "And I accept your apology, fair lady, and beg you think nothing more of it."

"Unless I've stumbled into one of those historical romances my mother enjoys so much, can we get on with the planning?" I asked. Without waiting for a reply, I continued, "How much does your insurance-scamming friend want in return for this service? I assume it won't come cheap?"

"No, it won't." Gunther grimaced, "He wants five million credits. He claims it's a reasonable fee for such a rush job."

"Tell him he can have three and a half million," Michelle responded immediately. "Be prepared to walk away if he doesn't agree, but accept a counter offer of four million if he makes it."

"Why bother?" I asked. "It's not like a million and a half credits matters to us either way."

"He won't know that and it's better for us if he doesn't figure it out," Michelle responded. "If he realizes we aren't budgeting our money, there's a chance he might figure out who is behind this whole thing. Your name and background have been all over the station for the last day or two, so it's not a big stretch." She turned to Gunther. "Does he know you're Matt's uncle?"

"Not to the best of my knowledge, but I approve of your caution." Gunther bestowed a smile on Michelle. "After all, the man could make quite a bit more than that turning us over to the authorities."

"Can you trust him to go through with his end of the bargain?" I asked. "I'm assuming he'll demand payment up front. Besides, we won't have time to stop and pay him afterwards."

"That's why I'll be supervising his operation," Gunther said. "Once he actually blows out the bulkhead, I'll run for the ship. It's also why I came back to the ship—I need a credit stick with the right balance to give to him."

We prepared two credit sticks, one with three and a half million on it and a second with half a million. Gunther took them and left to finalize the deal.

At Michelle's insistence, I searched for a list of psychics assigned to the Piscain Station Psi Corps office. That proved much harder to find than the office's emergency procedures, but I finally found it. As expected, they had a bunch of telepaths. Those are not only the most common psychics, they're also generally the most useful. The office had several empaths, a few telekinetics, two healers, three pyrokinetics, an astral projectionist, and one whose ability was restricted only to those with Top Secret clearance.

"Why would you want a pyrokinetic in a space station?" Michelle asked. "Isn't fire the last thing you'd want?"

Shrugging again, I said, "I don't know much about pyros. Maybe they can put out fires as well as start them? That would be really useful in this kind of environment. But I'm more worried about the astral projectionist. If she's on the station, they could send a message to another station without bothering with a messenger drone."

"But they already tried a drone," Michelle reminded me. "Why would they do that if the projectionist was in the office?"

"Maybe they're being sneaky or maybe she was resting after an earlier sending. I read somewhere that sending interstellar messages really exhausts an astral projectionist." I ran my hands through my hair in frustration. "There's so much we don't know and won't have time to learn before we make our move—what if we missed something vital?"

"Then we'll deal with it when we find it, babe." Michelle went back to rubbing my shoulders.

Grinning, I went back to massaging Michelle's chest. "Oh look, I think I found something vital. How should we deal with it?"

A soft moan escaped Michelle's lips. "Is there anything more you can get from Psi Corps' files?"

"Without taking some really big risks, no," I said.

"Then I'd like to test a new theory of mine." Michelle pulled me to my feet and toward one of the ship's cabins. "I think we won't get screwed during our rescue plan if we get well and truly screwed *before* the rescue."

That sounded extremely reasonable to me.

# PSI CORPS

**B**efore I realized it, someone was banging on the door of our little cabin. As I came awake, I felt Michelle stir in my arms. She stretched languidly, feeling lithe and wonderful against my body.

"Are you decent, Matt?" Uncle Gunther called through the door.

"He's a lot more than decent at this, Gunther," Michelle purred. "He's downright wonderful."

"Saints preserve me," Gunther muttered, "would it be too much to ask for the two of you to get your minds back on the task at hand and away from what's between your legs?"

As we rose and started dressing, I replied, "Our minds *were* on the mission. We've been strenuously testing Michelle's theory that if we're well-screwed *before* the mission begins, we won't get truly screwed *during* the mission."

Gunther was silent for a few seconds and then laughed. "Where were girls like Michelle when I was your age and going on pirate raids? Meet me on the bridge in a couple of minutes so we can go over the meager details of our plan."

As my uncle implied, it only took ten minutes to go over all of the details of our plan. Michelle showed us the plot she'd made for the movement of all of the naval vessels still patrolling the system and the best course the nav computer calculated for our escape.

"I've got the sensors feeding their scans into the nav computer so it can update our projected course based on the most recent data available." Michelle tapped on the nav controls the display sped through a projection of movement over the next several hours. "Assuming the navy holds to their flight patterns, which they probably won't once the decompression alarm goes off, our best bet is going to be wormhole delta."

Gunther nodded. "At least that one takes us toward the fringe rather than deeper into the Federation."

"You do agree that Matt should be our pilot, don't you?" Michelle asked.

"Hmph. I've been flying since before Matt was even a glimmer in his daddy's eye," Gunther grumbled, "and I've flown in more fights than he has."

Michelle blew out an exasperated breath. "That was twenty-five years ago, Gunther. Matt's younger, quicker, and his experience evading pursuit is extremely current."

"Yeah, yeah, you've been over all of that," Gunther said, waving a dismissive hand. "I agreed to it and will abide by my word."

While Michelle and Gunther bickered back and forth, I'd been scanning star charts. "Wormhole delta is a great choice, hon. I think wormhole beta should be our backup option."

"Why?" Michelle asked.

"Because delta leaves us two jumps from Ark's Landing," I said. "If we have to take beta, it'll only be three jumps."

Michelle clapped her hands together. "That's the perfect place for us, Matt."

"Why on Draconis is Ark's Landing such a great choice?" Gunther asked. "If that's the planet I'm thinking of, it was only colonized a decade ago."

"Yep, that's it, Uncle," I said. "It's perfect because it was a joint selection by both Federation and Fringe politicians—meaning it lies outside of the Federation."

"And," Michelle added, "we've got a very good friend who lives there. Nancy is a hero to the entire population, too, which means the local government won't just turn us over to the Federation. It will be good to see Nancy again."

"All right," Gunther nodded, "we go to Ark's Landing. It's just a waypoint for me, anyway. Once you and your friends are safe, I'll be off to free Tess."

I nodded. "Understood."

With as light a heart as possible in the circumstances, Michelle and I set out for the Psi Corps offices. Gunther waved and headed in the opposite direction. By station time, it was officially late evening, but the loading bay should have been busy around the clock. The travel embargo established by the navy really bit into the evening work shift. Every ship in the bay had been processed many hours ago. Now the crews just waited for word their ship was free to leave. It made for an uncrowded walk to the bank of elevators.

We shared the car with another man who did his best to unobtrusively check Michelle out. I could have told the man he was wasting his time. Jonas made sure his daughter was extremely observant. A half smile played across Michelle's lips every time the guy cut his eyes at her. I wondered if it was the attention she enjoyed or the idea that she was far better at surreptitiously watching people around her than the guy was. I suppose I could have read Michelle's emotions every time she gave that little smile, but everyone deserves their secrets.

When we reached the man's deck—a very crowded entertainment level—he motioned for Michelle to go first. I guess he assumed a woman dressed as she was couldn't be headed anywhere else. She smiled brightly and shook her head. He let his eyes roam her body and shrugged as if suggesting it was Michelle's loss.

As we rode on, Michelle asked, "Do you ever wonder what goes through a guy's mind when he watches me like that man did?"

"You said it yourself when we were on Rockville Station," I

replied. "To that man, you were a brief bit of fantasy. He's probably already forgotten about you."

"Oh, thank you so very much," Michelle said, affecting an indignant tone. "You know just the right thing to say to make a girl feel good about herself."

I looked into Michelle's blue eyes. "If it helps, *I* won't ever forget you."

"Yes, babe, that *does* make me feel better."

We reached our deck and sauntered down the corridor toward the Psi Corps office. Back on the ship, we'd checked the station layout around the office and discovered it was only a few meters from a small lobby. The lobby was deserted at this hour, but we acted like a furtive couple looking for a private place for a little necking. Any member of station security who saw us on a monitor would assume we were having an affair and move on. As a bonus, our cover involved me actually necking with Michelle.

Twenty minutes later, my comm buzzed. When I answered it, Uncle Gunter's voice asked, "Aren't you finished with dinner? We've got a lot of work left to do."

That meant everything was in place for our decompression. I gave the code phrase indicating we were in position and ready. "Something has come up. You'll have to go on without me."

Two minutes later, the station decompression alarm sounded.

All along the corridor, vid displays flashed the bright red words "Decompression Alert". The wail of the alarm rose and fell in time with the flashing message on the vids. Red arrows appeared on the walls and flowed toward the nearest decompression shelter. There were few people in the corridor, but none of them were panicking. Following procedures drilled into all space station citizens, they walked purposefully in the direction the arrows pointed.

The volume of the alarm dropped a few seconds later. A calm, synthetic voice announced, "This is not a drill. Decompression incidents have occurred in three sectors. For your safety, please remain calm and report to the nearest decompression shelter.

Station safety crews are en route to all affected sectors. Repeating, this is not a drill."

Michelle and I remained in the little lobby, out of sight of the people hurrying to safety. As the voice repeated its announcement, Michelle gave me a concerned look. "What is your uncle up to? I thought there was only going to be one incident."

"So did I, Michelle, but there's nothing we can do about that now. I suppose it will keep station security busy and make ordinary people more likely to go to the shelters." I stuck my head into the corridor and looked both ways. "The coast is clear—let's go."

Taking Michelle's hand, we walked purposefully toward the Psi Corps office door. I had hoped everyone inside would come pouring out when the alarm sounded, but also hadn't expected it. All big offices on space stations have their own shelters. Why should Psi Corps be any different?

Halfway to the office, a man and two women came around a corner and headed toward us. They were barely holding their fear in check; new citizens or visitors, probably. One of the women gave us a strange look.

"You're going the wrong way," she said. Pointing in the direction she and her friends were going, she continued, "The arrows are pointing that way."

"We work in an office nearby," Michelle said. "We're going to its shelter."

All three of the others stopped walking. "Thank God! Can we come with you? We're new here and—"

"I'm sorry," Michelle interrupted. "That's not possible."

"Why not?" the man demanded. "Our safety briefing when we came onto the station said we should get to the nearest shelter and that shelters have to let us in."

"That law applies to normal shelters," Michelle said with impatience, "not Psi Corps' shelter, which will be full of psychics."

"So what?" one of the women cried.

"You don't have the training necessary to withstand their abilities," Michelle said in an officious tone.

The man decided he'd had enough and took a menacing step toward Michelle. Knowing we had a very limited window to free our friends, I dropped my psychic shields and searched the area for fear. It was all around us, broadcast by people huddling in private shelters worrying about their loved ones, their lives, and their livelihoods. Hating myself for doing it, I drew as much of the fear into myself as possible in a couple of seconds, then pushed it into the minds of the three people before us. Their faces lost what little color they had and they stumbled back, raising hands as if trying to ward off a blow.

"Run!" I hissed urgently. "Follow the arrows or you're going to get sucked out into space where you'll die alone and terrified. Run for the shelter."

Panic overwhelmed them and the trio broke into a run. Watching them scramble around a corner, I released the rest of the fear I'd drawn in and said, "Let's go."

Michelle eyed me for a second then said. "Can your power detect Cassie and Kristin and maybe find some happiness to broadcast to them? They're smart girls and might figure out what you're doing. If they know we're coming, they'll be ready to help or run."

"Good idea, hon," I said and mentally switched gears to search for happiness. People assume disasters drive all sense of joy from people's minds, but they're wrong. Joy comes from all sorts of things—knowing your loved ones are safe, knowing you're safe, or even something as petty as getting out of a dreaded meeting.

I siphoned off some of those happy feelings then cast about for the young precog and the telekinetic. I had no trouble finding Cassie's mind among the crowd in the office. Despite her young age, she radiated calm. Not worrying about finding Kristin, I broadcast happiness into Cassie's mind. Some of the warmth and love I felt for the little girl went with the happiness. Realizing that was a far better way of alerting Cassie, I released the emotions I'd stolen and simply poured my own into her mind.

A few seconds later, Michelle gave a sudden start. Turning to me, she said, "Gene is sending messages to me. He says the office door is locked, but Kristin is working on breaking the lock. The whole office acts as a decompression shelter. We'll have to open an airtight hatch just inside the main office door, but that's all. As long as there's air pressure outside the hatch, we can open it."

Reaching for the office door's controls, I gave Michelle a questioning glance. She shook her head, indicating Kristin was still working on the lock. Seconds passed and still we waited.

"Gene says Kristin has never tried sabotaging a door lock before," Michelle reported. "It's taking her a while to feel out how everything works."

"Can't we just shoot the lock with a blaster?" I asked.

Michelle rapped her knuckles on the door lightly. "It's armored to stop exactly that sort of thing, babe. I know our schedule is tight, but just give Kristin a little more time."

Another minute passed as we just stood there. I kept looking in all directions, watching for any other stragglers or station security officers who might ask why we were just standing at the door. I kept a tap on all of the fear bubbling up around me, ready to draw some in and broadcast it at anyone who questioned us. When I caught sight of someone wearing a uniform rounding a corner twenty meters away, I drew in some of that fear. That's when Michelle reached out and opened the office door.

The airtight hatch was a couple of meters beyond the entrance. It had an old-style manual locking mechanism so emergency personnel could open it if the station's power was out. As I reached for the big wheel, Michelle caught my arm.

"Draw in as much fear as you can hold, Matt. We need to go on the offensive as soon as we open that hatch."

"How useful will my power be, Michelle? We already know there are a lot of telepaths assigned to this office and they'll all be immune to my power. They've probably got some psychic nulls like Zav, too."

"Just pull in as much fear as you can and then blast everyone in the office with everything you've got," Michelle replied. "We'll deal with the ones you can't affect when the time comes."

"What about Cassie and Kristin?" I asked. "They'll be affected, too."

"Cassie is the one who suggested it," Michelle said. "Gene and Mark are holding hands with them so they can shield them from you as much as possible."

I concentrated on drawing fear from all around me. In my short time doing this, I'd discovered some emotions can be tough to draw out of people—usually good ones they want to hold onto —but fear is easy to take. Even when fear is both justified and useful, no one wants to hang onto that emotion. Within a few seconds, I had a big, uncomfortable, squirming ball of fear occupying most of my mind.

Nodding to Michelle, I motioned to the hatch. She spun the locking wheel and then shoved the hatch open. I had just enough time to take note of the crowded office and the people turning toward the hatch. I grabbed Michelle's hand hoping I could spare her from the effects of my power.

Feeding all of my willpower and all of my own fear our rescue attempt would fail into my ability, I broadcast my stored fear at everyone before me.

I put all of my pent up anger and frustration at Psi Corps and the society which spawned it into my psychic blast of fear, adding my own fear for the safety of my friends, my wife, myself, and even my uncle. The results were...unexpected.

Eyes widening in fright, at least two dozen people shrieked in absolute terror. The eyes of more than half of those shrieking rolled back in their heads and they simply collapsed, unconscious. Everyone else in the office was affected by my mental onslaught. *Everyone*, including telepaths like Gene and Mark, who should have been unaffected, and psychic nulls like Zav, who should have been immune. Some of them stretched hands before them as if trying to ward off a blow. Some of them covered their faces as if they were too afraid to face this terror. Some of them simply turned and ran away from me. But every last one of them was affected in some way—with one lone exception.

A middle-aged woman standing at the back of the crowd stared at me. Her eyes were disturbing, blank and almost unseeing. I gave her a quick read, afraid I'd sent her into a catatonic state, and found nothing. It wasn't that I couldn't read her—her mind was wide open—but there was nothing in her mind to read. She was completely blank emotionally.

Holding hands with Michelle must have protected her because she neither screamed nor tried to get away from me. Instead, she murmured, "Damn, Matt, that's impressive."

Turning away from the puzzle of the unaffected woman, I called, "Zav, where are you? We've got to grab the kids and get out of here."

Off to one side, Zav stumbled forward. Bending over, he lifted the still form of Cassie. My heart leapt into my throat at the sight of the little girl. Then she moved, turning her head my way and smiling weakly.

"I knew you'd come," she said, her voice barely more than a whisper.

Behind Zav, Gene and Mark lifted an unconscious Kristin. The boys looked shaky but determined. Releasing my hand, Michelle stepped forward and reached her arms toward Cassie. Zav, who was also glassy-eyed, stumbled toward Michelle, ready to pass Cassie to her.

The only other movement came from the far side of the crowd of people, where a well-dressed older man pushed himself off from the wall. He straightened his jacket and flashed a predatory smile. "I knew you'd come, too, Mr. Connaught. People like you are very predictable. I did *not* know you'd be such a powerful psychic. To the best of my knowledge, no psychic has *ever* affected a null. Counting that traitor, Zavier Gordon, *you* affected six nulls. Six! Capturing you will more than make up for me not finding Gordon and his lot living on the station."

"Are you delusional?" I said, glaring at the obnoxious man who was obviously the office chief. "No one in this office is in any shape to stop us. What you just felt was a wide-spread blast. Anyone who tries to stop us will earn my displeasure and very personal attention."

"You misunderstand, Mr. Connaught," the office chief said, his smile widening. "You will surrender to me without a fight."

"Wow, you really *are* delusional," Michelle said as she reached for Cassie. "Come on, kids, we've got a spaceship to catch."

The office chief pointed at Michelle. "That one, Sadie."

The middle-aged woman's eyes moved from me to Michelle. My wife gave a sudden, surprised sigh and then collapsed. I rushed to Michelle, lifting her in my arms. Anguish shone in her eyes and she took short, sharp breaths. Her hands locked onto my arm as if holding on for dear life. I tried for a quick read of Michelle, but my abilities slipped and slid around whatever Sadie was doing to her.

"She's going to die, Mr. Connaught unless I order Sadie to release her." The smugness in the office chief's voice turned my stomach. "All you have to do is surrender. Once we have you properly secured, Sadie will release your wife."

My blaster was pointing at Sadie before I even realized I'd drawn it. "Tell her to release Michelle or I'll blow her head off."

"No, Matt!" Zav shouted, stepping between the middle-aged woman and me. "There's no telling what will happen to Michelle if you kill this woman while she's psychically connected to her."

"Listen to Zav, Mr. Connaught," the office chief said. "Surrender is your only real choice."

I lowered the blaster and looked back at Michelle. Her eyes darted about rapidly before finally meeting mine. With an obvious effort, she held them on me. Michelle's mouth opened and she fought to speak.

"I must say I'm impressed with the strength your wife shows, Mr. Connaught," the office chief said. "Once she's properly broken, she'll be an excellent incentive for your good behavior."

I ignored the man, leaning close to hear what Michelle was

saying.

"R-r-read...me...n-now."

Tears stung my eyes and my voice filled with anguish as I whispered, "I tried and I can't get through."

Michelle's head jerked left to right and back again. "N-n-no...t-take...out."

Could I pull this out of Michelle's head like I'd removed her fear when we abandoned our spaceship outside of Piscain Station? I couldn't punch through Sadie's power to read what Michelle felt, but maybe I could get around Sadie's defenses. After all, Zav told me I was the first empath he'd ever heard of who could draw feelings from people.

Reaching out with my ability, I found the slippery, impenetrable ball of Sadie's power. I tried simply yanking it out like I'd done with Michelle's terror, but the psychic ball slipped free of my ability's grip.

"You'd better make up your mind soon, son," the office chief chided.

Ignoring the man, I went after that ball of power again. This time, I used my own power to envelope the squirming mass of psychic energy. When my power fully engulfed Sadie's, the middle-aged woman gave a sharp gasp.

"What's going on? Is something wrong?" The confidence ebbed from the office chief's voice with each word.

"You said it yourself, John," Zav said, his tone light and conversational. "Matt's a very powerful psychic—only he's even more powerful than you realize."

Careful to keep my grip on Sadie's ball of power, I gently drew it out of Michelle, reeling it into my own mind. Once I had the thing in my own head, I found it much easier to keep it isolated.

With a loud gasp, Michelle sat up and said, "I knew you could do it, babe!"

"Noooooooo! She's *mine!*" Sadie's voice sounded rough, cracked, dry, as if she never used it, and the cry sounded just like that of a young child deprived of a favorite toy. "Gimme back!"

"That's not possible," John, the office chief, said, disbelief in his voice. "No!"

I stood and locked eyes with Sadie. I felt her fighting against me, trying to find some way to break free of my control. With every move I blocked, the woman grew more frantic. Spittle flew from her lips as she screamed her frustration.

"Looks like Matt has countered your living terror, John," Zav said.

"I admit he's surprised me, Zav," John replied, his tone returning to normal. "There's only one problem—he can't protect his wife forever. Once Sadie feeds on a mind, she can *always* find it again. This young man can't keep her out forever. When he drops his guard, that young woman is as good as dead." John's voice almost purred when he added, "But *I* can control Sadie, Matt. If you surrender, I will keep your wife safe. You have my word."

Never taking my eyes off of Sadie, I said, "Yeah, you'll keep Michelle safe until you want me to do something that goes against my morals—then you'll order this pathetic creature to attack my wife. Or one of my friends. You will always have access to someone I love too much to let Sadie take."

"Yes, Matt, I will." The smug tone was back in John's voice. "And there's not a damned thing you can do about it."

Michelle drew her own blaster and pointed it at the office chief. "I could simply kill you."

He laughed, a harsh and cruel sound, and said, "Then who would control Sadie? I trained her. Hell, I *raised* her. She obeys only me."

Michelle turned her blaster on the frothing woman. "Then maybe I'll shoot Sadie, first."

"While your husband is psychically connected to Sadie?" John's voice grew even smugger than before, something I hadn't thought possible. "Are you willing to risk your husband's sanity or his life?"

"Goddammit!" Michelle cried, her frustration evident, and lowered her gun. "I can't do it."

"I can," I said and shot Sadie between the eyes.

## A CHANGE IN PLANS

The compassionate part of my mind recoiled in horror as Sadie's head disintegrated. The protective part of my mind smiled in grim satisfaction as I removed a serious threat against Michelle. Then the effect of Sadie's death exploded through our psychic link, blasting through what few psychic defenses I could erect. I lost my hold on the ball of psychic energy I'd drawn from Michelle's mind and it joined in the backlash.

All light was driven from my mind. My eyesight failed and everything went dark—and not the darkness of everyday life. This was utter darkness, the complete absence of light, and all the more terrifying because I knew I was in a brightly-lit room. I felt as if I'd been sealed in a box and buried underground.

All sound was driven from my ears. Surrounded by dozens of people, some of whom had to be screaming or crying or retching in reaction to Sadie's death, I heard nothing. I couldn't even hear my own breathing or heart beating. Every sound of life was simply gone and beyond my ability to hear.

All feeling was driven from my body. I knew my hand was still wrapped around the blaster, but I couldn't feel the grip pressing against my fingers. I knew I stood on a solid floor, but I couldn't feel it beneath my feet. The heat generated from the packed mass of people inside the Psi Corps office was gone, as was the feel of the light breeze generated by the air scrubbers. I couldn't even feel the clothes on my body.

I wasn't just alone, I was completely cut off from everything and everyone. I was cast out of the universe and into a hell of absolute solitude. Words cannot express the desolation, the despair which overwhelmed me.

No man should ever face isolation so complete. No man *could* ever face isolation so complete. I had no defense against it. I tried hiding from it, but how can you hide from nothing? I tried running from it, but it engulfed me. I realized there was only one escape, one refuge from this horror.

I must die.

Death would welcome me with open arms. Death would banish the nothingness. Death would save me. Death would take me away from everything. Death would take me away from...

From far, far away, something tried to catch my attention. Something. Not nothing. No, some*one*. Calling from beyond the nothingness. Calling to me. Interfering with my death, my sweet, longed-for release from the depths of despair. Who could be so cruel?

I felt I should know who. I felt they were familiar, near, even dear. I felt...something...for this person. Something. I felt *something*. And I felt it for...her.

Beyond the desolation, beyond the emptiness, she called to me. Somehow, I knew she shouted, but it came to me as a whisper. "Matt! Don't do this. Don't leave me! God, please, I can't lose you!"

In the deep, dark distance something flashed. Something golden. Blonde hair. And, surrounded by the blonde hair, blue eyes which sparkled with love, flashed with anger, and spilled warm tears.

Warm. I *felt* something warm. I *felt* warmth splash on my face. I *felt* it roll down my cheek.

I concentrated on the voice, the vision, and the feeling. They were real. It was this isolation which wasn't real. The voice and vision and warmth were life and love and laughter and joy and passion and everything that made life worth living. They were *Michelle*.

With a supreme effort of will, I flew toward the sensations. Going to them, I went to Michelle. Reaching them, I reached Michelle. Embracing them, I embraced Michelle.

Light burst into my life, driving away the desolation and despair. Bright, blue, terrified, red-rimmed eyes stared into mine, mere centimeters away. Tears flowed from them, drops of love and loss which splashed onto my face. Her voice keened and her body shook with sobs.

I wrapped my arms around Michelle and pulled her into a deep kiss. She stiffened in surprise, then her body softened and she returned my kiss with desperate fervor.

"He's alive!" Gene proclaimed from somewhere nearby.

People cheered—far more people than the few we came to rescue. As those cheers rolled over us, Michelle's kisses roamed over my face as if she was tasting me to make sure I was alive.

"I was afraid I'd lost you, Matt!" she said, sniffing. "I was *so* scared. Don't you ever do anything like that again."

"I'll try, but can't promise more than that, Michelle," I said. "I will always willingly trade my life for yours." I caught her head between my hands and looked deeply into those beautiful, blue eyes. "*Always*."

"If there weren't other considerations, I'd happily let the two of you enjoy your reunion," Zav said, leaning over us. "But I suspect we don't have time for that right now."

Michelle and I climbed to our feet. I didn't remember falling, but I wasn't feeling anything for a while there and wouldn't have noticed. "How long was I out?"

Michelle shuddered. "Too long—close to fifteen minutes."

A pint-sized bundle of energy barreled into me and held onto me as if for dear life. "Th-thank you for not dying."

"You didn't know I was going to make it?" I asked Cassie. Her head shook back and forth, never pulling away from my chest. I tilted her head up and smiled at her. "How could I die? Michelle and I haven't adopted you, yet."

"Adopt?" It was John, the pain-in-the-ass office chief. "That girl belongs to Psi Corps—as do you."

Voices erupted from all around us, shouting down the man. I turned a puzzled look to Michelle and asked, "Okay, what did I miss? Why are all of these people suddenly on our side?"

"Not everyone is," she replied, a smile widening across her face. "The Psi Corps officers have been trying to take control ever since you shot Sadie, but the Psi Corps *psychics* aren't having any of it."

I looked at the faces arrayed before me. Perhaps a dozen of them wore sullen expressions. Hopeful expressions shone from everyone else. "Let me guess, we're rescuing all of the psychics?"

Michelle nodded. "Yep. We're striking one hell of a blow against Psi Corps with this one, babe."

"How many people have we got now, including us?" I asked, keeping my voice low.

"I don't have an exact count, but it's around thirty."

"Then we've got a problem, Michelle," I said, still talking quietly. "My uncle's spaceship can't carry that many people—the life support systems will be overwhelmed and fail before we reach another system."

"We can't just leave them to fall back into Psi Corps' clutches, Matt," Michelle replied.

"No, of course not," I said, my tone just as adamant as Michelle's. "Our timeline hasn't changed any, but we're going to need a bigger spaceship."

Pulling her comm unit out, Michelle said, "Then I guess we're about to find out just how good of a pirate your uncle really is."

For some reason, Uncle Gunther was less than pleased when Michelle explained the situation to him. "You need *what*?"

"A spaceship big enough to safely carry thirty-two people to Ark's Landing," Michelle replied, her tone as calm as my uncle's was over-excited.

"Why in God's name did you wait until *now*—less than an hour before we leave—to tell me this?" Uncle Gunther's voice rose another octave, something I'd have sworn wasn't possible.

"Because I thought bringing Matt back from the edge of death was just a little more important than calling fifteen minutes earlier than I am now," Michelle replied, her tone sliding toward acerbic. "I also took an extra minute to get an exact count, too."

"Are you being serious, Michelle? Is Matt hurt?" A touching level of concern washed away the hysteria in my uncle's voice. "How bad is it?"

"He's fine now, Gunther. It was psychic backlash, but now isn't the time to go into details." Michelle's tone was all business again. "We know this is a huge change in plans, but we can't just rescue our friends and leave two dozen other psychics in Psi Corps' hands. You know Matt will never agree to that, and I won't either."

Zav returned to the office lobby with several psychics trailing behind him. "We've got the office staff locked in a supply closet, Matt. As Michelle instructed, we stripped them bare first. John and one of the women had implants, but Kristin was able to break them telekinetically. She also broke the closet door's knob and lock."

I grinned at Kristin. "Good job, kiddo. With any luck, we'll already be in the wormhole by the time they get free."

Behind me, Michelle continued her conversation with my uncle. "Right, we need a ship big enough to carry us all and fast enough for us to get away from the navy."

"What, no requests for a gourmet chef, also?" my uncle replied, sarcasm fairly dripping from his voice.

"A chef is optional," Michelle replied. "We're ready to leave, now. We'll see you in the loading bay in about thirty minutes."

"Don't be daft, girl," Uncle Gunther said, "there aren't any ships down here that meet our needs. Come to the docking bay on level three."

Michelle gave Zav a look. "Do you know anything about that docking bay?"

Zav nodded. "Yes, indeed I do. It's the exclusive docking spot for the rich jerks and their fancy yachts."

"Access restricted, right? And they have armed guards?" Matt asked.

Zav nodded. "How did you guess?"

"Because I'm a rich jerk with a fancy yacht."

Zav winced. "I'm sorry, Matt. I didn't mean-"

"I know you didn't," Matt interrupted, waving it off. "Uncle Gunther, how are we going to get past the locks and guards?"

"Don't ask me. You're the man with two dozen psychics and Michelle the Amazon Warrior." In a very dry tone, my uncle added, "You got into a secret pirate base on Pegasus Station with a lot less than that."

"Your confidence in us is inspiring, Uncle," I replied. "How will we find you?"

"I'll find you. Now, get moving, be careful, and start planning your excuses now." Then Uncle Gunther broke the connection.

"Excuses?" Zav asked.

"For when we run into station officials," Michelle said. "A small group might dodge around them, but there's no way thirty-two of us can do that."

Zav nodded and looked down at Cassie. "I don't suppose you've had any useful dreams about this, young lady?"

The girl shook her head, sorrow written all over her face. "You know I'd tell you if I did."

Somewhere back in the crowd of Psi Corps psychics, a low voice muttered, "Fat lot of good she is if she can't see our future."

Cassie's face fell and she looked at the floor so we wouldn't see the tears I knew were forming in her eyes. Even without my ability, it was obvious Cassie felt responsible for anything unfortunate which she didn't predict. With my ability, I felt the girl accepting the muttered comment as the truth and blaming herself because she hadn't predicted any of this.

A look of pure fury set on Michelle's face and she shoved and pushed her way into the crowd of psychics. "Move. Get out of my way!"

She stopped in front of a tall man in his late twenties. Michelle only came up to the man's shoulders, but he took a short step backward when he saw the look on her face.

"What, exactly, is your problem?" Michelle hissed. "You spent the whole time I was trying to save Matt bitching that we were wasting time better spent getting away. Now you blame a twelve-year-old girl because she couldn't predict this exact series of events? How dare you!"

Rather than apologize, the guy doubled down on his stupidity. "And I questioned just how useful she is if she can't predict things that actually matter. It's simple logic. Maybe you should try that instead of this emotional outburst."

"Oh, you want logic, do you? Then try this," Michelle hissed. "Zav and the others are on Piscain Station because Cassie predicted Matt and I would end up here. She predicted we'd abandon our spaceship and come to the station in spacesuits. She predicted the search for us, which gave Matt time to figure out how to hide the two of us from detection. *And* she and the others are the *only* reason we came to this office. So *she* is directly responsible for *your* chance to escape from Psi Corps."

To my complete lack of surprise, the guy had a temper. Rather than respond logically to Michelle, he got angry. "Fine, the kid *was* useful, but that doesn't make her useful *now*. Not like I am."

"*You* are useful?" Michelle scoffed. "What, can you materialize spaceships out of thin air or something?"

"No, I'm a pyrokinetic." The man lifted his hands and flames licked around them. The other psychics backed away from him. "I could burn every last one of you to ashes in a matter of seconds. And *that* is a useful power for getting out of here."

Michelle dismissed the man's claim with a nonchalant wave of her hand. "If you're so damned powerful, why didn't you escape on your own years ago?"

The man's face turned red. He raised his arms and flames

spread from his hands to engulf them, also. "How can a *normal* like you understand what—?"

The crack of a blaster interrupted the man's tirade. The flames snuffed out as he stumbled back a step before collapsing. A few of the watching psychics screamed and all of them pushed away from Michelle.

Holstering her blaster, Michelle met the fearful gazes of the other psychics. "What? It was set to stun."

A collective sigh swept through the room and people stopped trying to get away from my wife. One of the other men in the crowd said, "Better add an unconscious guy to the excuses you're making up for station officials. Who wants to help me carry Ron?"

Before anyone responded, Michelle said, "No, he stays here. He's the kind of idiot who will try to take revenge on me for shooting him and end up blowing up our spaceship. He wanted me to let Matt die and he dismissed as useless the one person most responsible for this rescue."

The one who volunteered to carry Ron protested, "But what-"

Michelle spun around to face the man. "He. Stays. If you don't like it, you can stay, too."

The man put his hands up as if he was warding off an attack. "No, I want to go. It's just that-"

"Let's get one thing straight right now," Michelle said, her gaze sweeping across all of the Psi Corps psychics. "Until we're safely on a planet outside of the Federation, you do *what* you're told to do *when* you're told to do it. We won't have time to debate our decisions in a committee. If you can't accept that, you're free to go your own way. Is that clear?"

Heads nodded rapidly in reply.

"Good," Michelle said. "Now, let's get moving."

Michelle and I each took one of Cassie's hands and led the psychics on the first leg of their journey to freedom.

Kristin's deft work breaking the hidden mechanisms of the airtight hatch of the Psi Corps office set off murmurs of appreciation among the other telekinetics in the group. The teenage girl smiled and deflected their praise by motioning to Zav and saying, "I had a really good teacher."

Zav paid no attention to Kristin's comment and joined Michelle. "You two have made quite an enemy in John. He's as ruthless as they come and won't take the loss of Sadie lightly."

"What's the deal with her, anyway?" Michelle asked. "And how come I could talk to Matt when she attacked me, but he was locked inside his own head?"

"I suspect it's a question of power levels," Zav responded. "John saw you as the key to controlling Matt, so Sadie only used a fraction of her power on you. Matt, on the other hand, got the full brunt of it in backlash when he shot Sadie."

"My God, if what I felt was Sadie's power on stun setting what was it like for you, babe?" Michelle unconsciously slipped an arm around me and pulled me close.

"Hey, I'm still in between you guys," Cassie squawked and then she scooted out from between us to take Zav's hand. "Okay, now you two can get all lovey-dovey."

"Oh, that's very generous of you, Cassie," I said, pulling Michelle in for a quick kiss on the cheek.

Though Michelle directed her question to me, Zav answered it. "The only person who truly understood Sadie's abilities was John. She came to Psi Corps as a preteen. Her entire family died under mysterious circumstances and everyone assumed she killed them—which she obviously did. There was actual talk of putting her down-"

"That's what you do to dangerous animals," Michelle gasped, "not people."

"Why do you think I had to leave Psi Corps?" Zav asked quietly. "Anyway, John volunteered to train Sadie. For safety, he took her somewhere remote, far away from other people, and worked with her for years. When they returned, the girl was devoted to John and did everything he asked. From then on, John's ascent was rapid. Rumors circulated that he used Sadie to remove people blocking his way and the way of those loyal to him. John never denied those rumors, either. Office chief on Piscain Station is usually the last stepping stone to being named the head of the entire agency."

"So, not only did we embarrass this John person, Matt killed the weapon he held over everyone else's heads?" Michelle asked.

"Yes, exactly," Zav said.

"Michelle and I never do things by half measures," I responded as we came in sight of a bank of elevators. "But that's a worry for later. Is there an elevator large enough to hold all of us?"

"The mass transit cars on either end of the row can easily carry us all," Zav responded. "But they only go as high as level eight. After that, we'll have to switch to smaller, restricted-access cars."

Cassie skipped ahead of us, "I'll call the elevator."

The second the girl left our corridor and entered the huge elevator lobby, a man's voice rang out. "You there, little girl. Stop where you are!"

Cassie came to a sudden stop and looked off to her right. "Are you talking to me?"

"Of course I'm talking to you." A note of impatience crept into the voice. "Do you see any other little girls around here?"

Signaling everyone else to wait in the corridor, Michelle and I hurried toward the lobby. As we got close, Michelle called out, "Cassandra, come back here at once."

Cassie turned our way as Michelle and I left the corridor. Ten meters or so to our right, a pair of uniformed station security officers marched our way.

Looking back and forth between the officers and us, Cassie pointed to the officers and said, "I can't, Mom—that man told me to stop right here."

"Of course he did, Cassie. A decompression alarm sounded and it's his job to make sure silly little girls like you are safe." Michelle turned an embarrassed smile toward the two men. "In all the confusion, she just slipped away from us. Thank you for stopping her for us."

The officers' pace changed from a purposeful march to a more casual walk, but they kept coming our way. One of them said, "Just doing our job, ma'am, but I'm afraid we're going to have to report this. Ignoring a decompression alert is a serious safety breach."

"Is that really necessary, officer?" I asked. Turning a stern look on Cassie, I said, "Rest assured my daughter will be punished."

"Sorry, sir, but rules are rules." The two officers stopped a couple of meters away. If they got much closer, they'd see the mass of people in the corridor. The one doing all the talking pulled out a data pad. "Names and address, please?"

The second officer's eyes suddenly widened and he reached for his holstered blaster. "It's the Connaughts! They're-"

Michelle took one step forward and kicked the second officer under the chin. His head snapped back and he fell to the floor.

The first officer tapped his badge with one hand as he took a step toward Michelle. "Officers under attack! Send—"

My fist caught the officer on the ear. He stumbled to the side and tripped over his partner. His hand scrabbled for his blaster as he struggled for balance. His eyes widened in terror as Michelle drew her own gun. The crack of blaster fire echoed around the lobby as my wife shot both officers.

Gasps sounded from up the corridor, drawing an exasperated expression from Michelle. "It's still set for stun. Good God, just how bloodthirsty do you think I am?"

From the officer's badge, a voice called, "Backup is on the way, Ellis. What is your situation? Ellis?"

"Cassie, go summon the elevator *now*," I said and she took off for the elevators at a run. I waved to the others who were still huddled in the corridor, "This place will be crawling with station security in just a few minutes. If you don't want them dragging you back to Psi Corps, get going."

That got everyone moving, with several of them even breaking into a run. Running ahead of them, I drew my own blaster and made sure it was set for stun. Michelle and I trained our guns on the closed elevator doors, ready to fire if the approaching elevator carried security officers responding to the call. Thirty seconds later, the doors slid aside and revealed an empty car. Shouts and running feet echoed down all of the corridors as we rushed people into the elevator.

"Move all the way to the back. We don't have time for anything else," Michelle said, providing helpful pushes to anyone who dawdled too much. "Matt, get inside and see if you can disconnect this car from station security's control. As soon as reinforcements get here, they'll call for an elevator override."

I ducked inside and shoved my way to the controls. Of course, I had no tools and no way to open the panel. "Kristin, I could use some help here."

The girl hurried to me. "What do you need?"

As she asked that, the last of our people entered the elevator. Michelle was right on their heels. "Take us up, Matt."

Punching the icon for level eight, I said to Kristin, "Can you pry this control panel free? I need to get to the electronics behind it."

Shouts sounded from the elevator lobby as the doors slid shut. Kristin concentrated on the control panel as the car began a swift ascent. Sweat popped out on the girl's brow as she strained with something much harder to break than the delicate electronics she normally sabotaged.

Slowly, ever so slowly, one side of the control panel pulled out from the wall. Then the elevator jerked to a stop. Station security was in control of our car.

# ELEVATOR SHOOTOUT

My hands hovered next to the edge of the control panel, ready to grab it and yank it out as soon as Kristin's ability pulled it far enough away from the wall. The teenage psychic poured everything she had into the effort, the strain obvious on her face.

"How long is this going to take, babe?" Michelle asked.

"Too long," I responded as I searched my pockets for anything I could jam into the narrow opening and use as a pry bar.

"You heard what Matt said. Why aren't the rest of you telekinetics helping Kristin?" Michelle demanded.

A stir ran through the crowd of psychics at my back and four people stepped closer. No one said anything, but the gap between the wall and the control panel widened quickly. A second later, I jammed my fingers into the expanding gap and yanked with all my strength. With a metallic creak, the panel popped off entirely. At the same instant, the elevator started descending—no doubt toward a lobby full of heavily armed station security officers.

Pulling out my data pad, I reached into the control panel's wiring and grabbed the diagnostic connector. I plugged it into my pad and the elevator interface popped up on my screen. Flicking to the manual maintenance screen, I quickly locked the elevator in place. That control overrides everything else in the system, otherwise a tech working in the shaft could be hit by a moving elevator. The car stopped with a jerk and I returned to the main screen in search of the security controls. We had no more than a minute before someone in security figured out what I did and canceled it.

Michelle, her voice pitched low, asked the four late-arriving telekinetics, "Why did you wait so long to help Kristin?"

Her voice tremulous, a woman replied, "Because no one told us to help."

"No one *told* you?" Michelle said, her tone incredulous. "God in heaven, do you *want* station security to capture you and send you back to Psi Corps?"

"N-no," the woman stammered. "But we're not allowed to use our powers unless we're told to use them."

"That is a Psi Corps rule. They're the people you're running away from, remember?" Michelle all but yelled. Her tone changed and it was obvious she was speaking to everyone in the elevator. "In an emergency, you cannot simply sit around waiting for someone to give you orders. You've got to act decisively or we'll never get off this station. Is that clear?"

A chorus of assents followed. Their tentative nature drew an exasperated sigh from Michelle. I could easily imagine her casting her eyes toward heaven in a silent prayer for patience.

Into the quiet which followed, Zav said, "Michelle, you must understand that Psi Corps conditions psychics from a very young age. Unauthorized use of their ability leads to swift and severe punishment. I'm afraid it's going to take more than your impassioned speech to break that conditioning."

As the conversation took place behind me, I continued flicking through menu screens on my data pad. As expected, the security menu was password protected. I tried the default password—you'd be amazed how many otherwise secure systems never bother disabling that password—but whoever set this system up wasn't that careless. A little note even popped up stating the password would expire in eight days. That didn't help me, but it did give me a thought.

"Does anyone know how long the current chief of station security has been in that position?" I called into the silence.

When no one answered, Michelle said, "Let me check the station net. Maybe it will tell me. While I'm looking, do you mind telling me why this is so important?"

"The security menu is password protected *and* has to be changed on a regular basis. Based on what I learned from my hacker contacts, that second bit is very rare in menus like this one." While explaining, I worked back through the screens, looking for the admin menu. "The elevator control software is a couple of years old. If the station chief started after that, he may have instituted the password rules for security systems but probably didn't think of doing that for another department's controls."

"That's about as clear as mud, babe," Michelle muttered, still tapping on her pad.

"Short and sweet, your average elevator maintenance tech doesn't worry much about software security. After all, you've got to get inside the control panel to even access it," I explained. "If those password rules weren't in place when the software was installed, maybe they left the default admin password active. The thing is you only get a couple of tries with that password before the system locks you out. If the security chief has been around for more than two years, I'll look for another way to hack into the security controls."

"Found the info on the station chief," Michelle crowed. "Let's see, she took the job eight months ago."

"Good enough." I looked over my shoulder at the mass of people staring intently at me. "Cross your fingers and hope for the best."

I entered the typical default administrative username and password—'admin' and 'password'—and tapped Enter. The screen blinked once and then the administrator screen displayed. "I'm in!"

Everyone gave a relieved cheer as I tapped my way through

menus to the command most feared by system security personnel. I selected 'Reset to Default Configuration' then entered the administrator password again to confirm I had the authorization to do this. Why the system asked for a password I had to enter just to get to this screen, I don't know, but it's standard in just about every kind of control software I've ever hacked. Data scrolled rapidly across the screen for a few seconds and then the display returned to normal. I quickly changed the admin password, then accessed the standard elevator controls and directed the car to level eight. With a slight jerk, the car ascended.

"Can they track where the car is going, Matt?" Michelle asked.

"Not immediately. When everything reset, station security lost their connection with the car." I quickly accessed the security menu again, this time gaining access without the required password. "If someone is really clever, they might figure out what I've done. That's why I'm entering my own security password."

Seconds later, I exited the security menu. My passwords wouldn't stand for long against a good security person, but I only needed them to last another minute or two.

With the first crisis averted, Michelle once again turned to the psychics. "How many of you are telepaths?" A lot of hands went up. "Good. Can you scan ahead of us and tell us if anyone is waiting for us on level eight?"

Those with their hands raised looked uncertainly amongst themselves. Into the silence, Zav said, "They can learn how to do that, but I'm afraid they've only been trained to use their abilities on people stand right in front of them. For the rest of our escape, it will be easier if you simply assume their abilities are limited to what they can see." Zav nodded to the teenage boy who met Michelle and me when we entered Piscain Station. "I trained Gene differently."

"I'm way ahead of you, Zav," Gene said, his eyes unfocused. "I pick up six security officers waiting for us on level eight and varying numbers of officers waiting at the elevator doors on other levels. They've got their blasters trained on the doors and are authorized to shoot if we even look threatening."

While the elevator car wasn't badly crowded, even with thirty of us in it, there was no way we could get more than a handful of us out of the line of fire. The elevator rose quickly toward level eight, leaving little time for planning.

"Everyone get down on your knees and put your hands on top of your head," I barked. "Michelle, you and I will be right up front so the officers won't have to hunt for us." I caught Mark by the arm before he sank to his knees. "I need you next to me, Mark."

Mark nodded, understanding my idea immediately. The Psi Corps psychics had no idea what I was planning and that made them nervous.

"Is he going to attack the officers?" one of them asked. "Because I don't think that's a good idea."

Mark and I sank to our knees as the elevator slowed. Shaking my head, I said, "Mark is going to do what he does best. He's going to make friends."

The elevator stopped and the doors slid open.

Before the doors opened wide enough for us to see the officers grouped outside of the elevator, one of them yelled, "You are under arrest for assaulting a station security officer and violating decompression regulations."

The doors slid farther apart. The first two officers revealed by the widening doors knelt on the floor three meters away from the elevator entrance. Both of them had their blaster pistols trained on us and wore determined expressions. I couldn't see the power selector for their weapons, but I'd have bet the entire Connaught fortune the selectors were set to 'kill'. The officer issuing orders stood a meter behind them and was just coming into view.

"Put your hands on your head and..." The officer came into view as the doors kept moving apart. His face slowly transformed from the same determined expression worn by his subordinates to one of slack-jawed surprise when he caught sight of all of us on our knees and with our hands already atop our heads. His voice lost its authoritative tone as he lamely finished issuing his commands. "Um... Don't move."

"What the hell-?" a young officer blurted once he could see inside the car.

"Don't question it, boy," an older officer growled. "Remember, we don't *want* to shoot anyone."

"Hello, officers," Mark said, his tone bright and friendly.

There were seven men and women arrayed outside the elevator, not the six Gene reported. Considering everything he'd been through today, I thought Gene was doing well to get that close.

The security officers all turned their eyes on Mark. He wore a wide smile and, if he hadn't been kneeling right next to me, I'd never have seen the strain hidden by the smile. I suddenly realized I had no idea if Mark could affect so many people at one time—especially so many people who were already extremely suspicious of us. Telepaths mostly concentrate their ability on a single person, though I'd assumed Mark's charismatic ability was different. But what if a narrow focus didn't mean broader powers?

Zav must have seen the concern on my face from his place to Michelle's left. In a barely audible whisper, he said, "Mark can handle this as long as we don't dawdle or do anything stupid."

I gave a fractional nod in response as Mark continued his greeting. "We heard there were armed officers up here and didn't want any misunderstandings. But now you can see we're just a tour group. We were a long way from our ship when the alarm went off and are just trying to get back to it."

The officers exchanged glances among themselves and several turned questioning looks on the one issuing commands. Seeing this, Mark pressed his point. "I know we were supposed to go to the closest shelter, but we've all got friends and family on the ship. Besides, we weren't really sure where the closest shelter was. But we're almost back to level three, where we'll be out of your hair entirely."

Even as some of the officers gave 'that makes sense to me'

shrugs, one of the Psi Corps psychics muttered, "You told them where we're going. Just how moronic are you, kid?"

"Shut up, dumbass," Gene hissed back. "There's just one docking bay above this level. It's our only possible destination."

"What was that?" the leader asked, his expression softening but still suspicious. "What did those two say?"

"Oh, those two are always bitching at each other," Mark responded smoothly. "They're from rival families—sort of like the Montagues and Capulets."

The leader's attention returned to Mark, puzzlement replacing suspicion. "Who?"

"Um, the families in *Romeo and Juliet*, Shakespeare's most famous play." Seeing deepening confusion, he added, "He's an ancient Terran writer. We studied him in school."

"Now I *know* they're rich kids from a ship docked on level three," one of the guards murmured. "No one else studies that crap."

"Quiet, Barns," the leader barked. Coming to a decision, the man lowered his gun. "Lower your weapons, everyone."

Relieved smiles broke out among the officers as they brought their arms down though none of them holstered their guns. Then I spotted one officer frowning and looking at the leader. With a sinking feeling, I tried reading her emotions and got nothing. With a sinking feeling, I realized stress hadn't caused Gene to miscount the number of officers waiting for us.

Pitching my voice very low, I said, "Mark, we've got a psychic null out there."

"Sir," the null said, "you aren't buying this load of bull are you?"

"What are you talking about, Lindsey?" the leader asked. "These aren't the people we're looking for."

"The hell you say, sir," Lindsey said, bringing her gun up to bear on us again. "The pair next to the kid doing all the talking look a lot like the two fugitives we've been looking for. And why do they have a kid doing all the talking?"

"There's a perfectly reasonable explanation for all of this." Mark looked at the leader and his concentration deepened.

The uncertainty which had crept into the leader's expression cleared and a friendly smile replaced it. "That should satisfy even you, Lindsey. Now lower your weapon."

A look of disbelief flashed across Lindsey's face as similar expressions appeared on the faces of the other officers. "You can't be serious, sir?"

The five officers Mark used to have nodding in friendly agreement now looked confused. Mark's increased attention on the leader obviously freed their minds enough for Lindsey's objections to take root. A couple of them tentatively brought their weapons halfway up, not quite willing to point them at us yet but ready to do so.

Behind me, the psychic who questioned Mark's approach to calming the officers said, "Screw this!"

Heat flared behind me. Without turning around, I knew yet another pyrokinetic was off the rails. Was there something about that ability which turned those with the power into short-fused hotheads? Pun very much not intended at this point.

Turning, I saw a woman close to my own age with her arms wreathed in flames. She was raising her arms, no doubt preparing to engulf the guards in fire.

"Put those flames out, you idiot!" I yelled. "Don't you-"

Startled, the wavering security officers all brought their guns to bear on the elevator and looked to their leader for instructions. The leader did exactly what someone who lives on a space station does when they spot open and uncontrolled flames.

Pointing into the elevator, the officer in charge yelled, "*Fire!*"

Only a great fool or a pyrokinetic—from my recent experience, there's no discernible difference between the two—couldn't predict the security officers' response when a woman in the elevator caught fire. The instant I felt heat flaring behind me, I shoved Mark hard to the right and flung myself to the left, catching Michelle and bearing her to the floor.

The crack of blasters discharging was almost drowned out by the screams of the psychics packed behind us, but something in the massed fire sounded wrong. Something thumped to the floor behind me—probably the pyro's body—and the screams intensified.

Even pressed to the floor under my weight, Michelle drew her blaster and fired back at the officers. Shouting so I could hear her over the panic behind us, she said, "Only three officers fired. One is down. The other two are the ones kneeling right in front of us."

I was already reaching for my blaster before Michelle spoke. My draw was neither as smooth nor as quick as hers, but I brought my gun to bear as the two kneeling officers turned their attention on Michelle and me. My wife was quicker than any of us, snapping off a second shot before anyone else fired. One of the men pitched back, firing at the ceiling as his finger spasmed on the trigger. I was still aiming my blaster when the second officer lined his sights on me and squeezed the trigger.

And a blaster bolt did *not* punch a hole in my head. The officer's gun jerked up a few centimeters and his shot blazed over my head and into the back wall of the elevator. A comical look of incredulity flashed across the officer's face just before I shot him.

Though only a second or two had passed since the firing began, the remaining security officers realized something was wrong with their blasters. Two of them kept squeezing the triggers, apparently hoping the guns would suddenly start working. The other two, obviously more quick-witted than their fellow officers, dropped their blasters and dove for the guns dropped by the officers Michelle and I stunned.

The response Jonas trained into us when faced with multiple threats dictated what we did next. Without hesitation, I fired at the officer to our right while Michelle shot at the one on the left. The unconscious officers hit the floor and lay still.

The quick reversal of fortune stunned the two remaining officers into inaction. Still drawing on our training, Michelle and I smoothly changed aim and shot the remaining two guards.

"All of you, shut up!" Michelle shouted as she and I climbed to our feet.

As silence fell, we surveyed the scene in the elevator. The smoldering body of the pyrokinetic sprawled on the floor, three gaping holes burned into her chest. The elevator floor was visible through one of the holes and a quick look around showed one of the older psychics holding a burned shoulder. The third shot must have burned through the pyro entirely and wounded the man behind her.

I didn't need my ability to gauge the emotions of everyone in the elevator, but I used it anyway. The emotions of those I could read matched the expressions of shock and fear on their faces. We were close to losing control of the group and that was something we simply did not have time for.

"Let's go. Everyone get out of the elevator *right now*," I ordered. To emphasize my instructions, I started pushing people toward the elevator doors. I longed to draw the fear and panic out of everyone in our group, but I had neither the time nor concentration to do that right now. "Keep your eyes up, people, and don't look back when you get out of the elevator."

That's when I heard crying coming from just beyond Michelle. Turning, I saw Zav hugging Kristin. "It's okay, Kristin. Let it out."

The teenage girl had her eyes shut tightly, but tears still flowed from them. "I tried to move faster, Zav, but I couldn't. And then *she* lit up and it was t-t-too late!"

Michelle and I gave Zav a questioning look. Still patting Kristin's head, he said, "She started sabotaging the blasters as soon as the doors opened enough for her to see the guns. Alas, I never trained her on blasters, so she had to break several internal components before she was sure the gun wouldn't work."

"And she blames herself for what happened to the pyrokinetic," Michelle said in a soothing voice. My wife slipped an arm around Kristin's shoulder. "Come on, Kristin, let's get off this elevator."

Zav released the girl and the two of us followed Michelle and

Kristin off the elevator. I said, "She's also the reason that officer missed me, isn't she?"

"Yes," Zav responded. "She used her power to push the gun barrel up a few centimeters just before the officer fired."

"Does Kristin understand how many lives she saved just now?" I asked.

"Not yet," Zav said. "When she calms down, though, she'll figure it out. If she doesn't, we can always tell her."

I picked up my almost-forgotten data pad, commanded the elevator to descend to the lowest level of the space station and then disable itself, disconnected the pad, and slipped out between the closing elevator doors. In the lobby, I saw Michelle quietly talking with Kristin. Cassie, Gene, and Mark were gathered around the girl in a show of support. Then one of the Psi Corps psychics stepped in front of me, fear and anger written on his face.

"Two of us are dead and one of us abandoned—and it's all *your* fault!" he snarled.

"I did kill Sadie—something I'd do again to protect my wife—but you asked to come with us *after* I did that," I countered. "And you didn't protest even a bit when we left that other pyro in the Psi Corps office."

"What about Bridget?" At my obvious confusion, he added, "The woman in the elevator. You got her killed and you don't even know her name."

"Bridget's own actions got her killed. Or do you honestly think armed security officers are going to give a pyro the chance to burn them to death?" I brushed past the man, heading toward Michelle. "I don't have time for this. If you don't like it, stay here and surrender to those officers when they wake up." I raised my voice so everyone could hear. "That goes for the rest of you. You *chose* to come with us. If you don't like what's happening, you're free to stay here. If you still want your freedom, come with me."

Heading toward the restricted access elevators which could take us to level three, I glanced over my shoulder to see if anyone chose to stay behind. I wasn't surprised to see everyone—including the complainer—following me.

Before I got close to the new elevator's control panel, one of the telekinetics asked, "Do you need access to the controls?"

At my nod, all of the telekinetics—including Kristin—hurried past me. By the time I reached the elevator, the control panel was neatly peeled away from the wall. Leaning on my experience with the first elevator, I had sole command authority over the elevator in less than a minute. The doors slid open shortly after that, revealing a much smaller elevator car.

"How many of us can fit in the car, babe?" Michelle asked.

"The specs say it has a maximum occupancy of twenty, but designers usually err on the side of caution." I glanced at the car and then at the crowd of psychics. "Let's see if we can pack everyone in. I'd really rather not split up if we can avoid it."

Michelle took over, directing the psychics into the car. No one was comfortable by the time she finished packing them in, especially the lightest people. She had them sitting on the shoulders of some of the bigger psychics, but she managed to crowd everyone in with just enough room left for the two of us to fit into the car.

With the elevator's controls no longer restricted, I disconnected from the control panel and hit the icon for level three. The doors slid shut mere centimeters from my nose and then the car ascended swiftly toward our last stop on Piscain Station.

# AN OLD FRIEND

"Telepaths," Michelle called, "are you scanning our destination so we'll know what's waiting for us?"

The split second of silence following my wife's question told me these psychics hadn't grasped the idea of freedom yet. That's understandable, considering their upbringing, but very frustrating for Michelle and me. In our short time working with Psi Corps trained psychics, we only got the two extremes—they milled around like sheep when initiative was needed or went completely off the rails when milling around was the right choice. So far, the rail-jumpers were all pyrokinetics, but that could change at any moment. Besides, we still had one more pyro with us.

Several long seconds of studied silence passed while the telepaths looked ahead. Unlike the mass-transit elevator, our current car rose more sedately. Even so, we were passing level four before anyone spoke.

"Level three has its own private security force," one of the psychics said. "They're on high alert because of the decompression alarms and reports of blaster fire on lower levels."

"That's not unexpected," I said. "Okay, this is my area of expertise so let me do all the talking. Michelle and Mark, you're both with me."

"If you're doing the talking, what should I do?" Mark asked.

"See if you can make the guards receptive to my words," I responded. "Have you ever tried using your ability without talking?"

Mark blushed furiously. "Um, a few times."

Michelle arched one eyebrow. "How far did you get with those girls?"

"Why do you think I only tried it on girls?" Mark asked defensively. Michelle's snort spoke volumes and Mark continued in a subdued voice, "Some of them kissed me, but I swear I didn't try anything else."

"When this is over, you and I are going to have a long talk about girls and boundaries," Michelle said.

"Yes, ma'am," Mark muttered.

"Good." Michelle turned to me. "What about me, babe? Should I be ready to shoot if it comes to that?"

"Yes, but only if you can strike an alluring pose at the same time," I said. This time, Michelle arched both eyebrows, so I added, "With Mark projecting peace and brotherly love on one side and you looking...available...on the other side, maybe the guards won't look at me very closely."

The elevator slowed as it approached level three and I suddenly had one last thought. "Did anyone get the name of the guard in charge?"

As the doors slid open, a woman called, "Hoskins."

Beyond the elevator, half-a-dozen beefy men in impeccably tailored suits regarded the elevator with interest. One of them stepped forward and said, "I'm Hoskins. How may I be of assistance?"

Linking arms with Michelle and placing a friendly hand on Mark's shoulder, I led the three of us out of the elevator. "My assistant was just reminding me of your name, Mr. Hoskins. I'm rather terrible with names, even though I'm the one who asked the man who was in charge when we left for your name. I'm embarrassed to say I can't even remember *his* name now."

"You must mean Mr. Roman," Hoskins said.

The man's face and posture gave away nothing of what he was thinking, but I wasn't limited to visual clues. I read Hoskins' emotions and those of his companion guards. I picked up deception from Hoskins and wariness from the other guards. They were good men, well-trained and well aware that unexpected alarms caused confusion and created opportunities criminals exploited.

I looked past the guards at the door into the level three docking bay. "No, it wasn't Roman. Let me think..."

The same woman said, "The man's name was Wilson."

"Ah, so it was," I cried, smiling broadly at Hoskins. "Thank you, Elise."

"It's Linda," the woman replied.

I waved a hand over my shoulder, dismissing the complaint. "I asked Wilson for your name, Hoskins, in the hopes we could avoid all this tedious checking in when we returned. What with all of this walking around and then this decompression alarm, I am absolutely exhausted."

"No doubt, sir," Hoskins said, his tone polite but his posture and emotions were far from matching that tone. "You do realize station rules require all civilians to report to the nearest air-tight shelter?"

"Surely rules like that don't apply to *me*," I insisted.

"I'm afraid they do, sir. It's for your own safety."

Doing my best to channel a male version of Jayna, I asked, "But why must I tolerate a cramped—not to mention *public*—shelter when I have a lovely, comfortable spaceship right here?"

Hoskins offered a brief smile, raised a data pad, and asked, "What ship would that be, sir? And might I trouble you for your name? You do remember your own name, don't you sir?"

At that moment, the door behind the guards flew open and a uniformed man barreled through. The man wore the uniform of a private spaceship and captain's bars on his collar. Brushing past the surprised guards, the man stopped before me and snapped off a salute. "There you are, Mr. Malik. We've been quite worried about you, sir. Mr. Calley and your uncle sent me to escort you back to the *Southern Star*."

I beamed at Hoskins. "There you are, my good man. The ship is the *Southern Star*."

Hoskins frowned, certain something was amiss but unable to identify the problem. He checked his data pad, tapped an icon, and then looked at me. "Your name is listed as a guest of the *Southern Star*. Please excuse me for delaying you."

"There's nothing to excuse, Mr. Hoskins. Would that all people pursued their duties with such diligence as you." Waving to the ship's officer, I said, "Lead on."

The captain turned on one heel and led us past the guards and into the docking bay. The richly appointed docking bay was empty, with the exception of more guards and emergency personnel. No doubt all of the other wealthy folk were already comfortably safe in their own ships.

I smiled and walked beside the captain until no one outside of our group could overhear me. Even then, I kept my voice low when I asked, "This Mr. Calley—he wouldn't happen to have a son named Robert, would he?"

"Indeed he would, sir," the captain replied. "Young Mr. Calley is quite anxious to talk with you once we're all safely on board."

"What on earth is Rob Calley doing here?" Michelle asked. "It should be mid-semester at school and Rob always took his studies seriously."

Cassie caught up with us and asked, "This Robert—does he have red hair?"

I turned a surprised look on the girl. "Yes, he does. Have you seen him?"

She nodded. "Zav made me take a nap when we were waiting in the security office. I saw a red-haired guy standing in this docking bay—only I didn't know it was a docking bay or even that it was on this station. That's why I didn't tell anyone about it. Anyway, the guy with red hair was standing in here and looking real worried about something."

Michelle and I exchanged glances and both shrugged. She said, "We'll know more in a minute."

A minute later, the captain showed Michelle and me into a sitting room on board the *Southern Star*. Zav and the kids stayed with us while everyone else went with the captain. Inside the room, Rob was pacing back and forth like a caged animal. Uncle Gunther and Mr. Calley were seated and sipping brandy.

When we entered, Rob rushed across the room to us. I thought he was going to hug us or something, which struck me as a little weird. Rob and I were good friends, but we weren't demonstrative about it. Instead, he stopped short and looked a little embarrassed.

"I'm glad you're all safe," Then he turned to Cassie and smiled. "And I'm especially glad to finally meet *you*, Cassandra."

Rob's words bounced around inside my head for a second as I tried to come to grips with them. Before I even realized what I was doing, I fired up my ability and read my longtime friend. He was a jumble of emotions—excitement, trepidation, and relief. Then a shriek of pure excitement came from next to me.

"Oh my gosh!" Cassie cried. "You're a precog like me, aren't you?"

Smiling at the joy radiating from Cassie's face, Rob said, "I don't think I'm anywhere close to your power, but yeah, I think I have precognitive abilities."

"Is that why you're here at Piscain Station?" I asked.

"It is indeed, Matthew," Rob's father said. He spun the chair around so he faced me directly. "A few weeks ago, Rob came to me with a strange story. He said you were in trouble—no, he said you were *going* to be in trouble. When Rob told me he'd been dreaming about it for several nights in a row, I simply thought it was a subconscious reaction to you marrying Michelle."

"Huh?" Michelle asked.

"Rob used to have quite the crush on you, young lady," Mr. Calley responded.

"*Dad!*" Rob rolled his eyes. "That was years ago."

Mr. Calley waved off Rob's reaction. "My son was quite persistent, though, so I commed your father the next morning. When I brought up your name, he insisted we meet in person and ended the call. Thirty minutes later, Richard and Jonas showed up at our door, listened to Rob's story, and then told us that you and Michelle fled the planet the night before. More importantly, they told us to keep quiet about Rob's dreams or he might end up attracting Psi Corps' attention."

"They didn't tell us you were psychic, Matt," Rob said, "but after they gave that warning it was pretty easy for us to figure out."

"More importantly, when he told me we had to come to Piscain Station because you were going to need our help, I immediately ordered the *Southern Star* prepped for departure. We left before the morning was out. What with the alert out for you and Michelle, plus the decompression alarm, we've been quite worried about the two of you." Mr. Calley raised his glass to my uncle and grinned. "Honestly, I've never been so relieved to see a pirate as I was when Gunther showed up."

I gave my friend an inquiring look. "Rob, why didn't you just comm me about your dreams?"

"Probably for the same reason you never told me you were an empath," Rob replied.

I nodded in understanding. "I hate to say it—because I really appreciate what you've done—but coming to help us is the exact opposite of what Dad and Jonas advised. It probably put you directly in Psi Corps' sights."

It was Rob's turn to nod. "Yeah, that's why I'm joining your crusade against Psi Corps and the psychic impressment laws."

Michelle and I exchanged glances and then she said, "You do realize Matt and I have only *talked* about doing that, Rob?"

"You'll do it, assuming we manage to reach Ark's Landing safely," Rob assured us. "Mentioning that, we'd better get you to the pilot's seat, Matt, and get going."

"Me?" I asked. "Don't you already have a pilot?"

"Sure. He's great if you want to move a ship carefully through crowded space without spilling anyone's cocktail," Rob replied, motioning me toward the door. "I don't think he's the right choice for flying through the middle of a Navy task force."

Rob led me out of the sitting room and Michelle naturally fell in beside me. Over her shoulder, she told Zav and the kids, "Make yourselves comfortable. We'll check back with you once we enter a wormhole."

Davis, the *Southern Star's* pilot, wasn't happy with the decision to replace him. "I've flown you and your father for twelve years and suddenly you're going to replace me with this...this...*boy?*"

"Matt is quite an accomplished pilot, Davis, and he has practical experience with evasive maneuvers." Rob took pains to remain polite, but his tone was firm.

"What on earth are you talking about, Master Calley?" Davis managed to sound both offended and perplexed. "We're under orders to remain here until the navy gives us clearance to leave."

"I realize that, Davis, but our situation has changed. We need to leave now or we won't ever leave."

"I see." Davis clearly did not see, but he suddenly turned his attention on me. "If you're such a capable pilot, you surely won't mind answering a few technical questions for me?"

Rob opened his mouth to protest but I beat him to it. "Sure. Fire away."

Without another word, Davis fired off question after question. His attitude didn't soften even slightly as I rattled off answers about the maximum thrust of the main engines and the maneuvering thrusters, the ship's defensive systems, and its weapons.

After I answered the sixth question, I immediately fired off a question of my own. "Do you think the engineer can fake an engine malfunction? If so, we can go full burn right from the start and have some serious velocity building before the naval ships even pick us up on scanners."

"You're going to slag half of our dock doing that," the pilot said, his tone laced with disapproval.

"I know what I'm going to do to the dock," I growled, "but that's not what I asked."

"I'm a pilot, not the engineer," sniffed the man. "Why don't you ask *him*?"

"I will," I said. "Rob, I think it would be best if your pilot went to his quarters and stayed out of my way."

"Who do you think you are?" the pilot spat, his supreme act of willpower failing. "You can't order me out of *my* pilot's compartment."

"Actually, it's *my* pilot compartment," Rob said in a flat voice. "You're a good pilot, Davis, but what we're about to do is beyond your training and experience. Matt, on the other hand, has evaded determined pursuit three times in the last year. Please go to your quarters until we're safely away from this system."

His face a mask of fury, Davis rose stiffly and stomped from the compartment. Watching the pilot leave, Rob sighed, "I don't think Davis will ever forgive me for this." Turning back toward Michelle and me, he added, "I'll get Aarn, the engineer, on the comm for you, Matt."

A few seconds later, I found myself staring at a grizzled man while I explained my idea. The engineer frowned, rubbed his chin, and said, "It sounds a mite tricky to me, lad. What does Davis think o' the idea?"

My mind spun through half-a-dozen ways to tell the engineer that I'd sent the pilot to his quarters. "Well, ah, you see..."

When the engineer's frown deepened, Michelle leaned in front of me. Her voice breathless with admiration, she said, "Hi Mr. Aarn! Rob had to send Mr. Davis to his quarters because he got very snippy when Matt explained the plan to him. *He* says you can't fool Navy sensors, but *I* bet you can do it."

All I could see was a head full of blonde hair, but I readily heard the engineer's tone change from doubtful to paternal. "Well, far be it from me to let down such a pretty lass. When do you need it done?"

"I'm so sorry, but the sooner the better." Michelle let a little pleading enter into her voice. "You *can* do it, Mr. Aarn, can't you?"

"Of course I can, miss. Is five minutes soon enough?"

Very quietly, I murmured, "That's faster than I could have hoped for, so yes."

Her voice bright with excitement, Michelle cried, "Oh, that would just be *amazing*, sir. Thank you *so* much!"

"I'll get right on it, little lady."

The comm screen was blank when Michelle sat up. She wore an insufferably smug expression when she spun to face Rob and me. "Shouldn't you be doing some preflight checks or something, babe?"

As I busied myself with that, Rob asked, "How did you do that, Michelle? On his best days, Aarn is gruff, but you had him eating out of your hand."

"Men like Aarn will never admit it aloud—they may not even realize it—but they all have a secret desire," Michelle said. "They wish they had a daughter, a daddy's girl to gaze with wide-eyed wonder at their work. If a girl knows the right expression and the right tone of voice, she can get a man like that to do just about anything for her."

Continuing my preflight check, I asked, "God help me, is this what I can expect from our daughters?"

Her voice still smug, Michelle said, "No, babe, it's *much* worse when the girl really is your daughter."

"You're going to have daughters?" Rob asked in confusion. "Are you pregnant, Michelle?"

"Not yet, Rob," Michelle answered, "but Cassie assures us we're going to have at least two little girls. Assuming we get away safely, of course."

"Of course..." Rob muttered. "Um, congratulations?"

Four minutes later—a minute ahead of schedule—Aarn told us everything was ready in the engine room. Rob warned all aboard to strap in for acceleration and told them to keep their restraints fastened until we gave the all clear. The three of us also strapped in

—me in the pilot's seat, Michelle at the weapons controls, and Rob at the comm console—and I brought the engines online.

"Hang on," I said, "this is going to be rough."

Then I shoved the main engine throttle to maximum thrust.

With a lurch, the *Southern Star* tore free from the magnetic grapnels holding it to Piscain Station. Alarms blared all around the pilot's compartment as the ship's systems noted how close we were to the space station.

"*Warning! Main engines thrusting in proximity to man-made structure!*" The computerized voice was calm but insistent.

"*Alert! Manual control required!*" proclaimed a similar digital voice.

"*Alert! Engine malfunction! Ship's system cannot override engine thrust! Pilot required!*" a third electronic voice declared.

I kept a close eye on the sensors and our projected course as the ship pulled away from the space station. Our path looked clear for the next few minutes or so, giving us time to let our drama play out as if we hadn't set it in motion ourselves.

"Aren't you supposed to be piloting the ship?" Rob yelled over all of the alarms.

"Not yet," I yelled back. "Pilots don't spend a lot of time at the controls when a ship is docked and the engines are quiet. As long as it doesn't veer toward anything, I'll let the ship run uncontrolled for a while longer. That's what would happen if this was a real emergency."

"If you say so," Rob responded. "Hey, Piscain Station is hailing us. What should I tell them?"

"Don't respond yet. Communications officers don't spend a lot of time at their station when the ship is docked, either." I looked over at Michelle, who was watching her sensor screens intently. "Can you tell how much damage we did to the station before we pulled away?"

"I only have minimal information without running a sensor scan of the docking bay." Before I could say anything, she added, "And I won't do that because the weapons officer wouldn't be at her station, either. According to passive scans, our docking bay is now open to space."

"Don't worry, hon, the airlock into the rest of level three was closed and sealed. That's required during a decompression alarm, but I double-checked the airlock reading before engaging the engines."

"More people are hailing us," Rob called. "The two ships docked on either side of us want to know what the hell we thought we were doing and we've got a naval ship demanding an explanation, too. Do you want to talk to them, Matt?"

"No. The navy has my voice print. Michelle's, too, so neither of us can talk to them. Can you act the part of a panicked crewman who was closest to the comm when everything went wrong?"

"What happens if I can't convince them?" Rob asked.

"The *best* case is you, Matt, and all the other psychics get hauled back to Psi Corps and spend the rest of your lives slaving for them. Your father, Matt's uncle, Zav, and I end up in prison for our parts in this whole fiasco." Michelle turned a level gaze on Rob. "I'll lose Matt forever. Cassie and the other kids will never have the family they desperately want. That sort of thing."

"No pressure, then," Rob said.

Turning back to the comm console, he opened all channels. "Um, this is the *Southern Star*. We've, uh, got a problem. Or something. I think."

Four voices spoke at once, two of them sounding professionally calm and insistent while the other two alternated between fury and hysteria. After a few seconds, the naval officer bellowed, "*Silence!* This is an official naval matter now. The next civilian who speaks without my permission will have criminal charges filed against them."

The other voices immediately fell silent and the officer continued, "This is Lieutenant Cooper, communications officer aboard the destroyer *TFS Lancaster*. Explain your ship's actions, *Southern Star*."

Rob took a few seconds to compose himself, then blurted, "I

don't know! We just took off I mean, you know, whoosh but things don't whoosh in space but you know what I mean and a lot of people got thrown around and I think the comm officer got knocked out and I was the closest one to the comm and someone said answer the damn comm so I did and we're still waiting for the pilot and I hope he's okay because I don't want to die. Are we all going to die?"

When Rob paused and drew a breath, Cooper interrupted the torrent of words pouring from Rob. "Calm down, son. There's a whole navy task force out here who are going to make sure you and everyone on board that ship come out of this just fine."

His lungs once again full, Rob grinned and let loose another unending sentence. "Are you sure because no one is driving the ship or steering or piloting or whatever you do and what if it just decides to turn around and go back to the station and we end up crashing into the station and we all die and a lot of people on the station die because if the engine just lights up on its own why wouldn't the steering engines do the same thing or would that mean we'd spin around and around until the ship comes apart and we all die and pieces of the ship fly into the space station and wreck some of the other ships or something like that?"

Cooper tried to stem Rob's brilliant stream of consciousness run-on sentence but ended up waiting until Rob paused for another breath. "That's not very likely, son, so just sit tight while the navy works out what to do. And you really need to get *someone* into the pilot's seat before something else unfortunate happens."

In a normal comm exchange where the lieutenant wasn't trying to cram as many instructions as possible into Rob's pauses for breath, Cooper would have had time to consider what he was saying. He almost certainly wouldn't have even hinted that something 'unfortunate' might happen—especially not on an open channel.

A new voice came over the channel. "Piscain Station, this is the *Mary Sue*. We are making an emergency departure as a precautionary measure."

Another voice chimed in, "This is *Griffin*. We are also performing an emergency departure."

"For the safety of our passengers, *Serene Firefly* is disconnecting from Piscain Station."

"This is freighter *GCS-06*. We are departing with our cargo which is vital to a newly established colony."

Every time Lieutenant Cooper started speaking, another ship interrupted and announced their departure. By then, a dozen space traffic controllers on Piscain Station were arguing with all of the departing ships, struggling to establish some kind of order. They shouldn't have wasted their breath. The navy had held too many ships at the station when they were searching for Michelle and me. Those same ships were taking the panicked response from ships docked close to the *Southern Star* and using it as an excuse to finally get on with their run. Staying docked was too expensive and no one trusted the navy to consider a ship captain's bottom line and release them anytime soon. Minutes after our hasty departure, Michelle reported over two hundred ships under way from the station.

Amidst all of the confusion, no one even noticed when Rob calmly announced the *Southern Star's* pilot was flying the ship. He carefully added that the engines were still malfunctioning and the pilot was taking the ship away from Piscain Station for safety purposes. Twenty-two minutes later, our engines still burning at full thrust, the *Southern Star* entered wormhole delta and we were on our way to Ark's Landing.

# ARK'S LANDING

Once the gray mist of the wormhole engulfed the *Southern Star*, I finally took the time to check the star charts for our course to Ark's Landing. We had a six-hour wormhole transit ahead of us and an eight-hour journey across a system mostly dedicated to mining before making a final two-and-a-half-hour wormhole jump to Ark's Landing.

Contemplating the free time we had ahead of us, I suddenly found it all but impossible to keep my eyes open. When the pilot's console blurred before me, I realized just how thoroughly I'd over-taxed myself, both physically and psychically. "Rob, can you get the regular ship's crew to take over running the ship?"

"Sure," Rob responded. "I'll have to soothe our pilot's ruffled feathers a bit, but it won't be the first time."

I fished one of the credit sticks with a smaller balance out of my pocket. It held a balance of a little over one million credits. "Here. Split this up among the crew, both for their help getting us this far and for their cooperation getting us to Ark's Landing. That should settle a few of the pilot's feathers."

Rob whistled at the balance. "Yeah, I'd say so. What else do you need?"

"A room," I said.

"With a double bed," Michelle added.

Rob's eyes flicked back and forth between Michelle and me. A wicked grin spread across his face. "Of course. No doubt the two of you are exhausted from this ordeal and desperately need a little shuteye."

Michelle leaned against me. "Wipe that grin off your face Robert Calley. Matt and I really do just want to get some sleep."

Under Michelle's watchful eye, Rob's smile dimmed but didn't go out. "I have no idea what grin you're talking about, Michelle. I'll give orders that you're not to be disturbed. Come on, I'll take you to a cabin myself."

We took a moment to check on Zav and the kids. Zav was deep in conversation with Mr. Calley and Uncle Gunther while the four kids explored the *Southern Star's* state-of-the-art entertainment array. We begged off joining them, pleading a desperate need for sleep. My uncle and Rob's father gave Michelle and me knowing looks and I barely refrained from telling them that the two of us actually *did* use beds for something other than sex.

Zav, on the other hand, understood. "Honestly, Matt, I'm surprised you're still on your feet. You've pushed your ability beyond anything I thought possible—for you or anyone else. Michelle, make sure he gets all the sleep he needs."

"How will I know when he's rested enough?" Michelle asked.

Zav's expression shifted to match the ones Mr. Calley and Uncle Gunther wore. "When Matt responds...appropriately...to the lovely young woman in bed with him, I'd say he's fully recovered."

Gene and Mark snickered. Kristin, a dreamily romantic expression on her face, smacked them both. Cassie cocked her head as if trying to figure out exactly what everyone was talking about. Rob's father and my uncle guffawed and raised their wine glasses to Zav. To my surprise, Michelle blushed. I was too tired to even react.

"Come on, lovebirds," Rob said, leading us to a nearby cabin.

I had just enough energy to get undressed, leaving my clothes where they fell. Dropping into bed, Michelle and I snuggled together. I managed to give her one quick kiss before falling asleep in her arms. My dreams were troubled, filled with isolation and despair and loss. Finally, my exhaustion drove me into a deep and dreamless sleep.

When I opened my eyes, I found bright blue eyes looking back at me. Blonde hair framed Michelle's face and her tender smile. "How are you feeling, sleepyhead?"

I felt my lips form an answering smile. "Good. Really good. How long have I slept?"

"Twelve hours."

"What about you?" I asked. "How do you feel? Did you get enough sleep?"

"I'm fine, babe. I slept for about eight hours."

"Have you been laying around for four hours just watching me sleep?" I propped myself up on my elbow. "That sounds pretty boring."

"That wasn't *all* I did, babe." Michelle ticked items off on her fingers. "I took a shower. Then I composed a message for Nancy Martin on Ark's Landing and had it sent ahead in a messenger drone. I had some food delivered from the ship's galley. I ordered enough for two, so you could get something to eat when you woke up. *Then* I laid around watching you sleep."

I looked past Michelle to a heavily laden tray of food and then looked back at my wife. "That looks really good."

"It is," Michelle replied. "I nibbled a bit."

"I wasn't talking about the food," I said, "but I *do* feel like nibbling."

I lowered my head and Michelle gasped. "I like that kind of nibbling a lot, babe."

After that, we communicated in an entirely nonverbal manner. Finally, our bodies and emotions merged and drove the last vestiges of isolation and despair from my mind.

Nancy Martin met us when we touched down on Ark's Landing and brought along a group she introduced as her extended family. Lilla and Michelle—as formidable a pair of blonde beauties as I've ever seen—carefully appraised each other for an entire second.

Nancy actually held her breath until the two women smiled broadly and hugged like old friends.

"Ah, it appears we are going to be fast friends," Lilla's husband Raal said to me as our wives pulled Nancy into a big hug. "Thank God. I don't know what Nancy would do if our wives didn't get along."

"Nancy told us all about your trials on the *Ark 2*," I replied. "I couldn't imagine Lilla and Michelle *not* liking each other."

Raal regarded me for a couple of seconds. "You know, most people who meet us for the first time talk about our *adventures* on the *Ark 2*."

"Adventures happen to other people and can be enjoyed on a big vid screen from the comfort of your own living room," I responded. "Trials are what happen to the terrified people actually living through those same events."

Raal's polite smile widened to a friendly grin. "I must warn you, Nancy has told our two boys all about *your* trials rescuing your parents. They think you've had grand adventures and are going to pester you for stories."

"The stories about you and Lilla aren't enough?"

"We never fought hundreds of space pirates," Raal said. "By the logic of my eight-year-old son, defeating a computer and a handful of mercenaries just can't compare with that."

At that point, Michelle and Lilla drew Raal and me into their conversation. A few minutes later, colony officials guided everyone off of the ship and into housing the colony built specifically for newly arrived colonists. We settled in as best we could while waiting for the Colony Council to rule on our request for asylum.

To my considerable relief, the government of Ark's Landing granted us temporary asylum while they considered our case. Archibald Bransen, the Terran Federation ambassador, immediately applied heavy pressure on the little colony's government, insisting they extradite the whole lot of us back to the Federation. I expected no less from the ambassador.

Following the protocol established in the Ark's Landing Articles of Colonization, our asylum hearing should be open to the public and broadcast live across the colony. Ambassador Bransen immediately protested, insisting a closed hearing was in everyone's best interests. The man looked well on his way to convincing the Colony Council before Nancy shot it all down with one simple question.

When asked for her opinion of the ambassador's request by a local newsie Nancy asked, "What is the ambassador trying to hide from us?"

If Michelle or I asked the same question, it wouldn't have gotten much play. But it was Nancy Martin—the heroine of the *Ark 2*, the woman the colonists called 'Our Captain'—asking the question. The quote dominated the news cycle and the colonists responded, bringing their own pressure to bear on their council representatives. The morning after Nancy asked her simple question, the Council refused Ambassador Bransen's request. With the whole colony watching, our hearing began the very next morning.

The ambassador opened the hearing, discussing at length the dangers psychics pose to society and individuals. He gave graphic accounts of the Cairo Catastrophe and the aftermath, dwelling on the lives lost and ruined when an empath of vast power went insane. He followed those stories with a surprisingly accurate description of our arrival at the Psi Corps office along with everything which happened afterward. Piscain Station officials must have launched a drone with the details once our destination was known.

Jabbing a finger at me, Bransen thundered, "The most powerful empath discovered in the last four hundred years sits right over there. Do you truly want the ticking time bomb named Matthew Connaught free among your colonists? Do you truly want him reading and warping your emotions? Do you truly want another Cairo Catastrophe and the resulting death, destruction, and insanity that comes with it?"

Next Bransen swept his arm to encompass all of the psychics who came with us. "Do you want highly-trained psychics unleashing their powers on your people when Matt Connaught drives them insane? Should you be among the unfortunate survivors of such a psychic onslaught, will you be able to live with the knowledge *you* could have prevented it all by simply refusing their request for asylum?"

Bransen's voice softened and he smiled sadly at the council and us. "I hold no animosity toward psychics. These unfortunate people did not ask for this curse. But they are simply too dangerous to let roam free. The Federation has successfully contained the psychic threat for centuries. We can train them. We can protect you from them. We can make them safe, sane, productive members of our society. For the good of Ark's Landing *and* these psychics, let us take them back to the Federation. Let us take them back to our protective embrace."

Bransen gave a firm nod to the Colony Council, most of who were nodding as if in general agreement with everything he said. Bransen's presentation was masterful and emotionally persuasive, one which resonated with many on the council and among the spectators. My heart sank as my gaze swept over all of the thoughtful expressions around me. Then my eyes returned to my companions and my heart all but stopped beating.

Raal and Lilla wore contemplative expressions. Nancy nodded, deep in thought. As did *Michelle*. My vision blurred as my life lost all meaning. Gently, I took Michelle's hand and brought it to my lips.

In a low voice, I said, "I'll surrender myself to the Federation if that's what you think is best, Michelle. But only if they'll agree to leave Cassie and the other kids behind. Please tell me you'll take care of them and I'll go without complaint."

"What?" Michelle gasped, focus returning to her eyes. "Oh my God, Matt, no. Not in a million years will I let you do that."

"But you were nodding just now," I insisted. "You were *agreeing* with Bransen."

The council chair roused herself from her thoughts and said, "Mr. Connaught? Please rise and present your case for asylum."

Michelle rose, one hand pressing me back into my seat. "I will speak on behalf of those seeking asylum."

"Michelle, are you sure this is-" I began.

Her blue eyes bright with excitement, her smile wide and confident, Michelle whispered, "I've got this, babe. Trust me."

The council chair waved a hand. "Very well. Proceed."

"I'm speaking instead of my husband because I don't want anyone leveling accusations that Matt used his empathic abilities to sway the Colony Council. Even so, when I finish speaking I have complete confidence you'll grant our request." Michelle faced the ambassador, a patronizing smile plastered across his face. "When I finish speaking, I also have complete confidence Ambassador Bransen will retract his objection."

"I'm afraid that's not going to happen, Mrs. Connaught," Bransen said with absolute confidence. "I stand by everything I said."

"And I think you're going to change your mind with remarkable rapidity, Ambassador," Michelle replied. "Think back on what the ambassador said to us. His speech was rhetorically excellent, evoking all the right emotions at all the right moments. When he sat down, most everyone in the room was nodding in thoughtful agreement."

Michelle faced the council. "You on the council were nodding."

She spun to face the spectators. "You in the crowd were nodding."

She stepped in front of Raal and Lilla. "Both of you were nodding."

She turned to Nancy. "Nancy was nodding."

Michelle drew in a deep breath and let her eyes sweep across everyone, from the spectators to the council. "*I* was nodding."

A murmur ran through the crowd at that. Michelle's voice rose over it. "Yes, *I* seriously considered Ambassador Bransen's words. *I*, who have intimate experience with Matt's ability, was nodding. *I*, who gladly abandoned a life of luxury on Draconis rather than see him taken by Federation officials, was nodding. *I*, who put my life in jeopardy to stay with Matt, was nodding. *I, who would die rather than lose my husband, was nodding.*"

Tears flowed freely down Michelle's cheeks at this admission. "What kind of woman would turn against her husband, the love of her life, the center of her universe, because of an ambassador's speech?"

"I'll tell you what kind of woman would do that." Michelle wiped her eyes and turned toward Bransen. "A woman whose emotions were being manipulated by an empath."

The room was absolutely silent for a few seconds as everyone absorbed Michelle's words. Then Bransen jumped to his feet, shouting, "That's a lie!"

"Is it?" Michelle asked. "Have you ever been tested for psychic abilities?"

Face red and eyes bulging, Bransen sputtered, "Of course not."

"But you wouldn't object to being tested, would you?" Michelle asked.

With a force of will, Bransen regained his composure. "Alas, there is no psychic testing machine on Ark's Landing."

Michelle sighed in resignation. "So much for that idea... Just so we're clear, though, you'd allow testing for psychic abilities if it *was* possible?"

A self-satisfied expression on his face, Bransen said, "Absolutely and without reservation."

What can only be called a devilish smile spread across Michelle's face. "Are you aware, Ambassador Bransen, that telepathy and empathy are incompatible powers?"

"What on earth are you talking about?" Bransen asked, his composure slipping a bit.

"Telepaths cannot read empaths—at least not beyond a few surface thoughts—and empaths cannot read or sway the emotions of telepaths." Michelle turned to the one man on the council who wasn't nodding after Bransen's speech. "Sir, that means you're either a psychic null—someone who isn't affected by mental abilities—or are a low-level telepath yourself."

Bransen fought to regain the upper hand. "This is all very interesting, young lady, but I don't see how it applies here and now."

"Don't you, Ambassador Bransen? We've got a dozen or more telepaths in this very room." Michelle looked at the teenage boy sitting next to Zav. "Gene, can you read the ambassador beyond his surface thoughts?"

Bransen leapt to his feet. "I protest this abuse most vigorously!"

"Did you not just say you would agree to a test were one possible?" Michelle asked in the sweetest, most innocent voice she could manage. "I believe 'Absolutely and without reservation' is the exact quote. Are you a man of your word, Ambassador Bransen?"

With that last question, Michelle had Bransen and he knew it. He could either refuse Gene's test and watch his career as a diplomat come crashing to an end or allow it and deal with the consequences. Bransen's shoulders slumped and, his voice barely audible, said, "I am, of course, a man of my word. Proceed with the test."

All eyes turned to Gene as the teenager's gaze turned inward. He knit his brow as his concentration deepened. Gene broke into a sweat as he pushed himself harder. After half a minute Gene's expression softened and his eyes focused on the outside world again.

"I can't read him."

Pandemonium broke out among the spectators as Bransen's composure broke. As the council chair banged her gavel and demanded a restoration of order, the ambassador buried his hands in his face.

It took the council chair nearly a minute to restore order. When she did, the woman asked, "Do you have anything further to say, Mrs. Connaught?"

"I do, ma'am." Michelle met the eyes of each of the council members. "Consider what you've seen today and think about how many other psychics you may know—good people with some minor ability who have no idea they are different from you and me in any way. My friends are no different simply because you *know* they have abilities. Consider that when you make your decision today."

The chair nodded and then said, "Ambassador Bransen, do you have anything you wish to say?"

"Yes," Bransen replied, his voice thick with emotion. "I hereby retract my protest to the request for asylum."

By unanimous vote, the council approved our request for asylum.

I wish I could say the council hearing was the end of the matter, but it wasn't. Within days, a new Terran Federation ambassador arrived at Ark's Landing. She carried recall orders for Bransen, who very carefully met with the new ambassador outside of the embassy. As the embassy was officially Terran Federation soil, he would have been subject to Federation law inside the embassy's walls. No one was surprised when Bransen submitted an official petition for asylum to the Colony Council.

Diane Reynolds, the new ambassador, protested both Bransen's asylum and ours. Accusing Ark's Landing of harboring fugitives from Federation justice, she threatened an impressive array of economic sanctions against the colony. These ranged from import tariffs to calling in all loans issued to the government and colonists of Ark's Landing.

By the time the situation deteriorated that far, Dad and a whole raft of GenCo lawyers were on hand. They took point in combatting the threats, working in conjunction with the council. Hard as they fought against Reynolds, the lawyers could only manage delaying actions against her authority. Fortunately, we had a much greater ally on our side.

While Dad and the legal team were on the defensive, Magda—Michelle's mother—Mom, and Nancy went on the attack from a different direction entirely. As newsies flocked to the colony chasing the biggest story since the *Ark 2* was found, these three formidable women launched a massive campaign to sway public opinion in our favor.

Michelle and I were dragged in front of vid recorders, recounting tales of rescuing my parents and our desperate struggle to stay together after we blasted off from Draconis. We left Gunther out of the story entirely since real pirates never have been popular with the public. Besides, he had already taken a GenCo ship and left on his original mission.

When Mom and Magda brought Zav and the kids before the recorders, things really started going our way. Cassie was as personable and enchanting in vids as she was in person, but the real tipping point came several days after that broadcast. That's when the newsies' vid recorders captured Gene and his parents—carried to Ark's Landing in the fastest GenCo ship available—holding a tearful reunion at the landing field.

Mom followed the reunion by bringing all of the other psychics before the newsies, introducing them one by one, and then announcing GenCo would happily bring family members of any of the others to Ark's Landing. The newsies recorded seventeen more reunions, including ones for Kristin and Mark.

Seeing Cassie's popularity among Federation citizens, some enterprising newsie tracked down her parents and asked why they weren't already on their way to Ark's Landing. Cassie's father told the newsie, "We turned the little freak over to Psi Corps years ago. She's not our problem anymore." Then the man shut the door in the newsie's face.

The second Michelle and I saw that recording, we took Cassie aside and told her about it as gently as possible. Mom and Magda showed up just as we ended our buildup and told the young girl how her father reacted. Cassie listened quietly as we wrapped up. Michelle enfolded her in a hug and I sat ready to join in as soon as Cassie's tears began flowing. Only, there were no tears.

Looks of concern appeared on Mom's and Magda's faces. Mom knelt in front of Cassie and asked, "Are you okay, honey?"

"Sure," Cassie replied. "Why wouldn't I be?"

Her concern deepening, Mom said, "Doesn't it bother you that your family rejected you?"

Cassie finally showed a reaction, scowling as she spat, "*They* aren't my family. I was born to them, that's all."

"Um, that's sort of the definition of family, sweetie," Mom said, taking Cassie's hands.

"No, it's not," Cassie insisted. "Matt and Michelle aren't related, but they're still a family. They love each other and made themselves a family. I love them and that means they can be *my* family, too. Just like they said back on Piscain Station."

Magda cocked an eyebrow at Michelle. "What was it you said to her, Michelle?"

"We told her we'd adopt her," Michelle replied, obviously gearing up for an argument.

Magda smiled and said, "What a lovely idea."

Mom smiled and added, "I agree with Magda, but I'd like to ask Cassie one question."

"Okay," Cassie agreed, a broad grin on her face. In a stage whisper, she added, "I already know what you're going to ask, but I want to hear you say it anyway."

"That is going to take some getting used to," Mom said, her smile removing any possible sting from her words. "Well, Cassie, you know that Matt's father and I were prisoners of the pirates from the time Matt was thirteen until he was twenty. That means I missed watching and helping him grow from a boy into a man. But if you're willing, I would dearly love to watch and help *you* grow from a girl into a woman." Tears started rolling from Mom's eyes, but she never released Cassie's hands. "How would you like having Matt as a *brother* instead of a father?"

"Oh, then Michelle would be like my sister. I'd like that a lot." Cassie paused for just a moment as if considering exactly what to say next and then she said, "Mom."

The next few minutes involved a lot of hugs and tears and smiles. When everyone settled down, I tapped Cassie's shoulder and said, "Just because you're my sister now, don't think you can get out of babysitting for the girls when the time comes."

Mom and Magda exchanged startled glances before turning

very intense looks on Michelle. Then Magda asked, "Is there something you should have told us, Michelle?"

"I'm not pregnant if that's what you mean, Mom," Michelle replied. "At least, not yet. But Cassie has already seen two daughters in our future. I can only guess when they'll be born based on how old we looked in Cassie's drawing, but it's probably in the next two or three years."

That set off a new round of hugs and tears and protestations from each of our mothers that they were too young to be grandmothers.

Adoption on Ark's Landing proved a pretty simple procedure, especially given the vid of Cassie's father. The news of the adoption was wildly popular in the Federation and marked the end of the Federation's attempts to strong-arm the colony into returning us all for trial. Popular opinion was heavily on our side, especially since all of the psychics were on a planet outside of the Federation. While our story was popular, it wasn't enough to bring about an end to the psychic impressment laws. But at least we had a firm foundation on which to build that support.

Safe from the Federation at last, I felt a knot of tension I never even knew I had melt away as Michelle and I relaxed in our room. I shared my feelings of relief with Michelle and discovered she felt the same thing. I pulled my wife close and let our emotions flow between us.

"Too bad we don't need to get intimate for you to share your emotions with me anymore," Michelle said.

"Yeah, but when have we ever let that stop us?" I asked and began unbuttoning Michelle's shirt.

## THE STORY CONTINUES...

Matt's and Michelle's story continues in
*The Fugitive Snare*.

In the meantime, you might enjoy *The Counterfeit Captain*, the first
book in the Captain Nancy Martin series.

If you enjoyed *The Fugitive Pair*, please post a brief review.
Reader recommendations are the best advertising.

# ABOUT THE AUTHOR

 Growing up, Henry worked at the usual range of menial jobs before ending up in software development. In between the menial jobs and the IT jobs, he achieved some small fame as the writer and co-creator of the small press comic book titles Southern Knights and X-Thieves. In 2006, Henry also took up the mantle of professional storyteller. He performs regularly throughout the state of North Carolina and has recently released his first book of children's stories.

Henry has been a fan of science fiction for as long as he can remember. He has loved space opera and planetary romance since the beginning, that is why his science fiction novels end up in those subgenres.

Henry currently lives in Raleigh, NC, with his wife, son, two cats, and lots of imaginary friends all clamoring to tell him of their adventures.

www.henryvogelwrites.com

# ALSO BY HENRY VOGEL

**Science Fiction Novels**

*The Lost Planet*

*Fortune's Fool*

*The Scales of Sin & Sorrow*

*Scout's Honor*

*Scout's Oath*

*Scout's Duty*

*Scout's Law*

*Scout's Training*

*Hart for Adventure*

*The Fugitive Heir*

*The Fugitive Pair*

*The Fugitive Snare*

*The Counterfeit Captain*

*The Undercover Captain*

*The Recognition Run*

*The Recognition Rejection*

*The Recognition Revelation*

**Illustrated Children's Book**

*I'm in Charge! and Other Stories*